WHISPERLIGHTS

By Brendan Myers

Arcana Elements

Arcana Elements is an imprint of Arcana Creations.

Cover design by Pat Bellavance with art elements under license from Shutterstock.com

Editing by Marisol Charbonneau

Legal Deposit, Library & Archives Canada, March 2025

ISBN 978-1-7778589-4-0

www.arcanacreations.com

Acknowledgements

I thank Melinda Reidinger and her family, for opening their home in Bohemia to me again while away on their own travels. This is now the fourth book of mine whose first draft was part-written on their kitchen table; it is perhaps no accident that much of Summerland looks like Bohemia. I thank Helli and Xavi, who kept me in the very best of spirits during that time. I thank Erin Jamison and Lauryn Jamison, who provided much-needed inspirational encouragement, at the precise time when I needed it. I thank producer Melissa Hays, my publishers and long-time friends Pat Bellavance and Marisol Charbonneau, and my long-suffering editor Jordan Stratford, for believing in my work.

I give my deepest gratitude to everyone who supported and uplifted me during the early months of 2023, my *annus horribilis*. If the crafting of this story was part of my healing, still I might not have made it without you.

Table of Contents

This book is dedicated to everyone
Who loves adventure stories, because they love life.

First Light: Summerland

§ 1.

The flock of swallows gathered over a pasture beside the village and became a man. He stood in the field for a moment, regarding the dozen houses in the village before him and noticed the yellow paint on the walls and the red roof-tiles. Above them gathered the ominous grey clouds of a coming storm. He pulled his home-spun woollen cloak and hood against the first wave of rain.

Are you sure about this one?

The voice floated in the air near him in a tone rich with youthful worry, and elderly care.

"Indeed, I am," said the traveller in reply, brushing his hair out of his eyes.

But she is so young – only twelve!

"She won't be twelve forever," the man said. He noted which houses had lamps burning in their windows, and which ones had dogs in the yard. "And if she is to become who I believe she can be, she must pass her first test tonight. Come tomorrow, and it may be too late. You know what's coming."

You're taking a greater risk than usual with this one.

"No more than the risk you once took with me," he said.

Alas, I remember it well.

The traveller grinned and made a quiet chuckle. He took up his walking-stick, and crossed the gap in the hedgerow, entering the village.

§ 2.

When Athena heard the first growl of distant thunder, she climbed the ladder to the attic and threw open the windows. Her family's cottage was built on higher ground near the edge of the village, giving her an excellent view of most everyone's rooftops, the valley beyond, and the oncoming storm… low, heavy, and dark.

The first flash of lightning jumped from one cloud to another. Counting heartbeats, Athena waited for the sound of its thunder to measure its distance away. Each heartbeat was a league: the distance she could walk in about an hour. One heartbeat, then two, then three, and – *there*! The deep drum-roll of thunder. The first flash was three leagues away.

There – another flash. Count the heartbeats again. One, and two, and – *yes*! It's coming closer.

As the first drops of rain speckled Athena's face, she spotted the flock of swallows, swooping and twisting about the village, peering into the windows, and darting through the barns. She smiled seeing them, though thought it unusual for them to be so active in the rain.

Then she saw what became of them when they gathered in the field. She gasped.

Athena's mother climbed up the ladder to join her. She brought a honey-roll and broke it in half for the two of them to share. "I used to do this as a little girl, too," she said.

"I just saw a flock of birds turn into a man," Athena told her mother. She pointed to the pasture and said, "Just over there."

Mother looked. "I don't see anyone," she said.

"Come out with me… we'll find him!" Athena said.

"Not in this rain," Mother decided.

"But what if he's lost?" Athena asked.

The next clap of thunder was a knocking on the door – three heavy blows that rattled the cupboards and windows. Buddy, the dog, barked at it. Athena snapped around to face her mother.

"Maybe that's him!" Athena said.

They slid down the ladder and made for the front room, finding Father already there. He was loading the gunpowder into his musket. In his rush, he spilled some of it. Buddy sniffed at it, found it unpleasant, and returned to barking at the door.

Three more heavy knocks. Athena looked between her parents for guidance and took a step away.

"Don't answer it," said Father. "Could be bandits."

"In a storm like this?" asked Mother. "More likely, one of the neighbours."

"Every bandit in the world knows that good folk will open their door to a stranger in the storm," Father said. "And as soon as you do, they press a gun to your heart and demand all your money. You hand it over and they might kill you anyway. That's the way of things, these days. We all have to be bandits just to survive."

He moved to a window to try and get a glimpse of whomever was out there. But all he could see was a vague shadow of a figure with a long scarf and a walking-stick.

"What if it was you, caught in a storm, and nobody opened the door!" Athena countered.

Two more knocks, louder and more insistent. Buddy barked at it again. Athena put her hand on Buddy's head to calm him and moved to the window. She tried to catch a glimpse of the visitor. All she could tell, through the rain-washed glass and the semi-darkness, was that the visitor had trouble holding on to his cloak as the wind and rain pelted him. Another lightning flash and, in the same moment, a thunderclap. The storm was in its full fury over the cottage.

"We have to do *something*," Athena said.

Mother and Father, caught up in their own argument with each other, paid Athena no attention.

Another lightning flash, another thunderclap, and Athena could bear the indecision no longer. She opened the door.

There, framed by the blue-grey glow of the storm in the twilight, stood the stranger who fell to the earth from the sky. He was a little taller than both Father and Mother. His hair was blonde, greying at the temples, and unkempt and drenched and tussled by the weather. His scarf and cloak were full of patches, and sun-dulled colours; perhaps it was as old as he was. His belt had numerous pouches and purses attached and his forearms bore many scars. Were those from long distance travelling or perhaps also from fighting? As soon as he stepped into the light, Buddy trotted to his side, tail wagging, smiling, and relaxed. The man knelt down to offer Buddy a gentle petting.

"Good evening friends," said the visitor, smiling. Despite his roughshod appearance, his voice was clear, warm, and gentle, making his rough cloak seem like the fine-spun linen of a scholar.

Father clicked the mechanism of his musket to warn the stranger to come no further.

"No need to be afraid," said the visitor, without flinching. "I have no weapons. Well, I've a walking stick. But I'll leave it outside. Might I rest with you until the storm passes?"

§ 3.

The family sat him near the fire where he could dry his clothes. They gave him a meal of baked wild pork in olive oil and garlic, a honey-roll, and a mug of ale. Father kept his wheel-lock pistol close at hand. His gaze remained skeptical and alert.

"My name is Dubhdarra Muirthemney," said the visitor. "I've been on the road a long while now. Feels like it's been an age of the world! And no one has shown me the kindness you have shown tonight. Not for a very long time."

"Our village is too small to have an inn," said Mother. "So, putting you up ourselves is the least we can do."

Father, sitting at the head of the table, said "The little one here says you fell from the sky."

"He did!" Athena exclaimed, delighted. "There was a flock of birds, and they flew together on edge of Gull Narveson's cattle field, like a little whirlwind, and turned into him!"

Father faced his guest and said, "You must have troubled the birds where they were sheltering from the storm?"

"As it happens, I was right there," Dubhdarra said, with a smile growing on his face.

"You see!" Father said to Athena, proud of himself.

Athena glowered at Dubhdarra, to demand a clarification. He responded with a kind smile and a wink.

Mother asked, "Perhaps you could tell us where you're from? Your name; it's Kellslandic, isn't it?"

"It is," the traveller confirmed.

"My grandfather came from Kellsland," said Mother, relaxing a little. "As a refugee from – well, it could have been anything. But we've never been there ourselves."

"It is an interesting place," said the traveller. "They say more ghosts and more fairies live there than anywhere else in all of Summerland."

"That's a reason never to go," said Father.

Athena said, "Have you ever *seen* the fairies? Or a haunted house? How long have you been travelling? You must have seen all kinds of amazing things!"

"Indeed, I have," Dubhdarra said, smiling to Athena. "Trees that sing the sunup, on midwinter morning. Giants, on the slopes of the Sunward Mountains. Gemstone flowers, flying islands, candy-fruit falling like rain!"

Mother smiled, thinking the visitor's words were a little bit of fun for Athena's benefit. Father rolled his eyes but Athena leaned closer, eager to hear more.

"But the most amazing sight I've ever seen," Dubhdarra said, "is a family who took in a stranger on the road, on a stormy night. Such people could save the world, you know."

Mother grinned and rose from the table. "I'm afraid the only spare bedroll we have is a child's size. It was Athena's, from when she was smaller. We can put it here by the fire, if you like."

Father added, "And in the morning, you'll be on your way?" His posture told Dubhdarra he expected the answer to be Yes.

"Come the sunrise, I shall trouble you no more," Dubhdarra promised.

§ 4.

When Athena rose in the morning, Dubhdarra was already gone. His bedroll was stowed at the foot of the attic ladder. In the kitchen, the dishes and cutlery were clean, the tablecloth washed, and the floor swept. Their pantry baskets were full of bread, strawberries, jostas, cucumbers, and bundles of green onion stalks. Their flour-jars and olive oil bottles were refilled to the brim. A vase of fresh cut flowers perfumed the room. Buddy had his nose deep in a full dish full of fresh kibble. The morning's warm sunshine in the windows blessed everything with yellow-golden light. Father and Mother traded astonished looks.

"Strawberries... in springtime," Mother marvelled. "Strawberries don't come into season for months!"

Father traced his fingers on the tops of cupboard doors and under the hob. "No dust," he said, with widened eyes.

"And look at these flowers," said Mother, picking up the vase. "Fresh roses – six months early."

Athena said, "I told you letting him in was a good thing to do."

"Still, he could have been anyone," Father grunted. To Athena, he said, "Now get to your morning chores."

Reluctant, Athena took the empty wood-bundle from the fireplace and went to the meadow to collect sticks and twigs for kindling from the edge of the forest. Buddy the dog followed, nosing about the ferns and tall grasses for the scent-marks of rabbits or deer.

The meadow, still damp from last night's rain, smelled of springtime – the headiness of the living soil, and the richness of pine and cedar. The last streams from the spring meltwater ponds trickled down in their annual paths, sometimes pooling in depressions and sinking into the earth. In the forest, the trilliums had returned – their delicate white petals carpeted the thin soil between the rock stacks and the clefts.

On the crest of a hill, Athena spotted the visitor some distance away, with his scarf and his walking-stick. A white-tailed deer stood by his side. It seemed to Athena that Dubhdarra and the deer were deep in conversation, understanding each other as any two people could do.

"Dubhdarra?" she called out to him.

The deer looked her way, startled. Dubhdarra calmed him with a pat on his neck and a kiss on his forehead. He waved for her to join him, and she bounded up the hill.

When she reached him, he knelt on one knee in order to feed a rabbit with something he took from a pouch on his belt.

"Dubhdarra!" she called to him.

The animals scattered. Dubhdarra's smile grew to see her. "Young lady Athena!" he replied. "Come! I'm glad you found me before I got too carried away by the road."

"Is it true, what you said?" she asked. "Trees that sing? Candy-fruit falling from the sky?"

"Every word," Dubhdarra confirmed. "And especially what I said about people who take in strangers in a storm. I know it was you, who opened the door for me."

Athena studied him for a moment. "Who are you *really*?" she asked.

"Oh, I'm just a lonely traveller in his middle years, taking the long way home," he said, still smiling and looking out across the valley. A wistfulness crossed his face. Three, perhaps four, rows of hills rolled away to the distance, quilted with woodlands, hay fields, and pastures, fading into blue as they approached the horizon. It seemed to Athena that he could see all the way to Kellsland, hundreds of leagues away; perhaps past the world entirely, and into what might lie beyond. She reached out to touch him, but withdrew her hand, unsure if it was permitted, nor even if it was safe.

"Don't be afraid," said Dubhdarra, noticing her hesitation. "Well, not of *me*. Plenty enough other things in the world might be dangerous. But as for me..."

He reached into one of his belt pouches and withdrew a small wooden figurine of a winged rabbit. He crouched down to her level to offer it to her. "Take this and keep him safe. Consider it my thanks for welcoming me into your home last night."

"What is it?" Athena asked.

"If you're ever in trouble," Dubhdarra explained, "*serious* trouble now – the kind of trouble where the lives of your loved ones are in terrible peril – you can ask him to come and get me."

"It's just a wooden carving," Athena complained.

"Aye, it is. And I'm just a traveller," Dubhdarra said, with a wink.

She smiled, understanding his real meaning.

"Only three times, mind you," Dubhdarra warned as he rose to his feet. "After the third time, he'll be too tired to do it again, and I'll have to bring him home."

"Three times, I understand," Athena promised.

Dubhdarra gave Buddy a friendly tussle and a treat from his pocket. Then he took up his rucksack and started away. "I have to go now," he said. "There's so much more of the world that I have to see! And even a lifetime as long as mine is not enough to see it all. Isn't that wonderful? It means there will always be something to surprise me."

He grinned, tussled Athena's hair, and took up his walking-stick. He laughed as he walked away, happy with what he had done that morning, and with what may lie ahead. Buddy ran with him for a while, until Dubhdarra gave him a treat from his belt-pouch and sent him back to Athena.

She watched the strange traveller go until his path took him beyond a bend in the valley, and out of sight. Buddy nuzzled her leg, and she rubbed his neck and his belly. The swallows raced and swam about the meadow, barely higher above the ground than the stalks of yarrow and wild lavender, chasing the flies, playing with her. Lifting her gaze, Athena gathered the world into her heart. There, the hollow hedgerow that led to a perfect swimming spot, where a stream met the river. And there, the clearing in the forest with the best mushrooms, where she once hid under a blanket to see if the fairies would come to harvest them. The corner of the pasture where the wild cherries grew, what a gift to find them ripe in high summer, and not yet taken by the birds!

Meadows, hedgerows, forests, and waters: playgrounds, teachers, and stories.

Her Summerland.

But from the valley below, where her village lay in its nest between the hills, there rose a column of black smoke.

§ 5.

Athena found Father at the door of the house, surrounded by a team of soldiers. They wore long red overcoats, black breeches and tricorn hats, with belts hanging from their shoulders to carry muskets, pistols, cartridges, and swords. They smirked like schoolyard bullies with rich fathers – men who knew that no matter what they did, they would never feel the consequences.

Down the lane, closer to the centre of the village, two of the cottages were on fire.

Father aimed his pistol at the face of an officer. But not a single twitch of concern registered on the officer's expression. The man was calm and unimpressed.

"Mister Kildare, you should have read your discharge papers," said the officer.

"I did my service already, Colonel Crave," Father insisted. "You can't call me up again. I'm too old for the infantry – I have a family now!"

"We're calling them up, too," the officer said. "Our records say you have a daughter... where's she to, now?"

"She's only twelve years old!" Father howled.

"Old enough to work in the kitchen," the colonel said.

Athena ducked behind a tree. Months ago, when the first talk of war reached the village, Father had told her that no king in Summerland would want a girl on the front lines of a battle, and therefore she was safe. Still, the officer's power made her shiver. She had heard some of her father's stories about his wartime experience. Ancient temples and palaces smashed down by cannonballs with people still inside, whole cities set on fire, and digging trenches in muddy fields, while starving. They were enough to convince her, even at her young age, that she wanted nothing to do with army life. Looking around, she saw those stories unfold before her eyes. Soldiers took her neighbours, people she had known her whole life, and bound their wrists, bagged their heads, and pushed them onto wagons. The captives struggled and screamed, but the soldiers either ignored them, or bludgeoned them with the butts of their muskets. The crunch of broken bones shocked Athena's ears. Dogs ran out to protect their people, snarling and barking, but the soldiers gutted them on their bayonets, and kicked them aside. Waves of smoke from the burning cottages thickened in her nose and stung Athena's eyes. Someone, she didn't see who it was, fired a shot. A soldier fell. Four other soldiers ran toward the sound and released a barrage of musket-fire. A moment later, they pulled a body out of a cedar hedge. Blood pulsed from him with the last beats of his heart.

Athena ducked her head into a nearby shrubbery to vomit.

"If anyone else puts up a fight," Colonel Crave announced to the whole village, "he'll get the same. Now! We are looking for four more families. They know who they are. And if those families stay hidden from us, we will set fire to another house!"

No one moved; no one emerged from hiding.

"Well, then. You did this to yourselves. I have nothing to do with this at all," the colonel said. He made a gesture to his underlings, ordering them to act. They saluted him, and then threw burning torches into the windows of two more houses.

With slow and reluctant movements, three men emerged from a house. They hugged their children and their wives and presented themselves to the officer.

Athena felt a hand on her shoulder; she jumped with nervous tension and tried to run away.

"Athena!"

The voice belonged to her mother, but she felt no less tense.

"Come, they'll burn down the whole village if they can't find you," Mother said.

The soldiers lifted her on to a wagon beside her parents. The driver whipped the horse, and the wagon moved down the road away from her home, friends, and village, and away from her meadows, forests, and stories... her entire world.

§ 6.

The army camp held more people, and more different kinds of people, than Athena had ever seen before. People were marching, running, carrying barrels and pulling wagons, shouting orders, starting fistfights over an accidental jostling. From the parade ground in the centre, there fanned out various paths and avenues, some leading to storage depots, some to firing ranges and training courses, and some to rows of tents and cabins. Every path overflowed with people at work.

Athena and her family slept in a tent, with three other families from the village, in bedrolls laid on the bare soil. A small fire in the centre of the tent filled the air with smoke that stung Athena's eyes and seeped into everything. When she thought everyone else in the tent was asleep, she crept to Mother's side and touched her shoulder. Mother opened her bedroll for her, and Athena crawled inside with her.

It was the safest place in the camp to weep.

§ 7.

The sudden peal of a trumpet announced the sunrise. Soldiers scrambled out of their tents, yawning, complaining, and swearing. The noise filled Athena's tent and pulled her out of a dream.

A soldier's head pushed through the tent flaps. "Time to get up, you monkeys!" he shouted. "Work to be done."

Athena rolled over and covered her eyes with a stocking, to pretend she was still asleep.

"Come on, Athena," said Father. "This is how it is now."

Athena pulled the sock off her eyes and got up. "You talk like you're *fine* with how it is now," she said.

"No, I am not fine with it," Father said. "But what do you expect me to do? For all we know, this is what the gods wanted for us, and it's part of their plan. Maybe something good will come of it, that wouldn't have happened otherwise."

"Like what?" Athena asked.

Mother and Father exchanged wearied looks. Father said, "We'll have to wait and see."

Athena scowled at them, but did not know how to reply.

The family trudged along the path to the camp's head office to receive their work assignments. To Athena, everyone they passed on the way was ten feet tall. Soldiers, officers, tradesmen, and others whose role she didn't understand would bump into her and warned her to stay out of their way, if they noticed her at all. Looking for a landmark, she saw a flagpole rising above the sentry towers. Its banner was blue and featured a roaring wolf's head wearing a white crown.

The duty officer sent Athena to the kitchen where the head cook welcomed her with a scoff and a grunt. "Got a name, kid?" he asked.

"Athena," she told him.

"Understand this," the cook said. "At breakfast, lunch, and dinner, you're here to work. If you slack off, show up late, or go missing, I'll thrash the hide off you! The rest of the time, I don't care what you do. You ken me?"

"I ken you," she replied.

"And smile when you serve the soldiers," the cook ordered. "They're working hard to keep this country safe from the tyrant-king of Stagsland. Smiling is the least you can do in return."

The cook put Athena at the counter where the soldiers queued up to take their lunch. She ladled the hot soup from the cauldron and into their bowls, and smiled for each of them. The soldiers grinned and smirked when they saw her.

"A new recruit!" said one of them. When she poured his soup, he grabbed her wrist and pulled her close. "But I'm hungering for something else. Know what I mean?"

Athena tried to pull away, but the soldier's grip was too strong. Her smile, frozen on her face, became a confused plea for help from anyone nearby.

Help came when another child came up from the kitchen, carrying a new cauldron of soup to the counter. "Hey! You wanna *wear* that bowl of soup? Leave her alone," the boy told the soldier.

"You're a bold one," the soldier said, smirking at the boy. He let Athena go, but he winked at her as he walked away.

"Sylvano!" said Athena, recognizing the boy. "I didn't know they picked you up too!"

"They took the whole sodding village," said Sylvano.

Athena reached to her breast and clutched the little wooden rabbit which hung there on a leather string under her clothes.

When she finished washing the cauldrons after lunch, the cook sent her out of the kitchen, with a warning to return in an hour to begin preparations for dinner. She explored the camp, in search of a corner, or a hole – or any other place where she could hide for a while. Finding an unfinished patch of the wooden fortifications that surrounded the camp, with a hole not quite wide enough to squeeze through, she checked all the sight lines. The paths were thick with the marching of boots and the clanking of weapons and armour. At any moment, a dozen pairs of eyes looked her way. Were she to attempt escape, she would be caught in no time.

But what about the night?

She returned to the hole in the wall after dark. Putting out the lamp she carried, she checked the sight lines again. This time, the only thing she needed to worry about were the sentries doing their rounds. This gave her a minute or two between their passing to tug on the loose planks. A nearby stack of crates gave her a hiding-place for when the sentry passed her by. In three such rounds, she had a space large enough for her young frame to clamber through.

Beyond the fort there lay a moon-bathed meadow, and a treeline some hundred paces away or more. It was too far to run without being seen. The sentries on the watchtowers would pick out her shape in the darkness and raise the alarm. Even if she did escape, she didn't know the way home. But sitting with her back to the outer wall, she had just enough freedom to do what she had risked a beating from the cook to do.

She took up the wooden winged rabbit, and held it in both hands close to her face, and whispered into its ears: "Can you hear me? I'm in trouble. They've pressed our whole village into the army. I found a way out, but there's nowhere to go. I don't know the way back home. And I can't leave Mam and Da behind. You said I could call to you if I needed help. So, I'm calling. I don't know what to do!"

As she whispered into the figurine's ears, she noticed a spot of ground near the treeline, brightened by fireflies in many colours. A rabbit stood there, raised on its hind legs, regarding her. She sat up, but dared not make another move, lest she startle the creature. The rabbit remained still, his ears perked, his eyes attentive. The cloud of fireflies grew, like a carpet over the meadow, expanding into the depths of the forest beyond, shifting in their colours as they moved.

"Dubhdarra?" she asked.

At the sound of Dubhdarra's name, the rabbit hopped away through the tall grass. Before he left her sight, he sprouted a pair of wide wings from the fur on his back and took to the air. He flew straight into the sky, kicking with his hind legs with each flap of its wings. His silhouette disappeared into the moons, and out of sight. All was dark again, but for the many-coloured fireflies. A wisp of cool air breathed across the meadow.

"Dubhdarra?" she called again.

But the sound of his name drew no further magic from out of the dark. Athena sat on the ground again and kept a vigil until she fell asleep.

A hand on her shoulder awoke her. She looked around. The gold of the early morning touched the treetops and the edges of the camp's wooden ramparts. Dew slicked the grass around her, making her shiver.

"Good morning," said a warm and familiar voice. "Strange place to sleep."

Dubhdarra crouched by her side.

Athena reached out to hug him. "Can you take me and my family back home?"

Dubhdarra examined the fortifications, taking note of the sentries and their arms. None were looking his way; Athena wondered if he had done something to make sure of it.

"I could," he said. "But there isn't much left of it. No one lives there anymore. You won't be any safer. And the army would come looking for you."

"Why did they do it!" Athena howled. "We weren't a threat to anyone. We were nobody's enemy. Why did they have to take us here? It's not fair!"

Dubhdarra sat against the wall beside her. "You're right, you know. It's *not* fair."

Athena didn't expect him to say that. "My mam used to say that everything that happens, happens because that's what the gods wanted," she said. "And that they reward the good and punish the bad. But – I don't see anybody being punished for stealing my whole village! Sometimes I wish I could walk right up to the Gates of the Morning and make the gods *explain* themselves. Why do people do such horrible things? Why don't the gods stop them?"

Dubhdarra regarded her with curious admiration. "Why don't you ask them?"

Athena sat up straighter; here was another thing she had not expected Dubhdarra to say. "My da says you're not supposed to talk to the gods like that," she told him.

Dubhdarra smiled. "Sometimes, adults would like their children to remain children all their lives."

"You've explored all over the world, right?" Athena asked. "Have you been to the Gates of the Morning? Is it just a story? Or is it, like, a real place you can visit?"

"Yes, I have been there," Dubhdarra said, his smile growing wider. "It's on an island called Dawnland, which is part of the Scatterlands, beyond the Great Eastern Sea."

"Take me there!" Athena demanded.

Dubhdarra sighed. "Ah, but I'm sorry to say, it's not the kind of place where anyone can *take* you. You have to find the way on your own. But if you're intent on finding it –"

"I am, I absolutely am!" Athena insisted.

Dubhdarra's gaze somehow both softened and hardened. He *knew* things, Athena surmised; and he was afraid for her. But he was also proud of her.

She straightened her spine. "So how do I get there?" she asked.

Dubhdarra grinned. "It's obvious, isn't it? Follow the sunrise! And when it's dark, follow the Whisperlights."

"The Whisperlights?"

Dubhdarra nodded. "I believe you saw them last night."

Athena remembered the multi-coloured fireflies that surrounded the winged rabbit.

"They will guide you, but they will also *test* you, as the journey itself will test you," Dubhdarra said. "You'll have to be ready for anything."

"Test me...how?"

Dubhdarra looked to the distance and frowned. "I'm sorry, Athena, but I cannot tell you."

Athena sighed and pouted for a moment. "Anything you *can* tell me?" she asked.

Dubhdarra's smile returned. "Everything you need to *prepare* for the journey, you can find in this army camp here. Supplies, equipment, weapons... and training. And bring a few friends with you. You don't have to do this alone. Choosing the right friends is, in fact, your first test. I believe there's a young man who works in the kitchen with you, and he's lost his home, too."

"What, Sylvano Rizio? I can't be seen with him; his mother's a *strega*!" Athena said.

"And how do you think *he* feels about that?" Dubhdarra asked. "Maybe he would like to ask the gods a few questions, too."

Athena knew Dubhdarra was probably right, but she didn't want to admit it.

Dubhdarra cast his gaze to the distance, choosing his next direction. "It's a beautiful morning, isn't it? A journey like yours should start on a day such as this. It feels somehow *fitting*." He returned the little wooden figurine of the winged rabbit, pressing it into her hands like a commitment, a sacred trust. "I hope you find an answer for your question, Athena. I really do. The whole world deserves an answer."

Then he rose and walked away.

"I can call you again, right?" Athena called after him, holding the rabbit. "Two more times?"

"Two more," Dubhdarra confirmed.

A goldfinch landed on his shoulder. He bade her good morning, and gave her some seeds from his pocket, as he walked into the sunrise.

Athena examined the rabbit figurine in her hands for a moment, tracing its texture in her fingers, smelling it, wondering about it, gathering its meaning into her mind and making it real.

The hole in the wall behind her remained open: its jagged sticks and boards were the teeth of a hungry cave-bear, waiting and ready to swallow her. The marching boots and shouting voices of the camp became its growling. Athena faced it, quivering. She felt sure this monster would crush her and destroy her... and take pleasure in it.

If Dubhdarra spoke the truth, that dark and denticulate hole in the camp wall was the first step on the path to the Gates of the Morning. Somewhere inside it, a trumpet played the Reveille, the sound that summoned the soldiers out of their beds and to the parade-ground for their first hour of training. The officers barked their orders and the low drone of hundreds of other morning voices rose in the air. Athena's other choice was into the forest – no less full of danger, and all the more unknown. She took a deep breath, to hold a moment alone in the cleave between the forest and the camp; between everything she had lost, and everything she might become.

Then she tucked the rabbit figurine into a pocket beneath her skirt, and climbed through the teeth of the monster, and into the camp.

Once through, a column of soldiers marched by. She quickly withdrew behind some crates and shrubbery, waiting for a moment to dash away unseen. To her surprise, they paid her no attention – their boots tromped along the gravel in perfect lockstep, and their eyes looked forward, never down. The danger was not in being seen, it was in getting trampled.

She stepped out of her hiding place and strolled down the path, taking care to stay out of everyone's way. She arrived at the kitchen in time for the morning chores.

"Meet me at my tent tonight, after dinner," she told Sylvano. "Can you get away?"

"Easily," said Sylvano. "What's this about?"

§ 8.

When her father returned to the tent at the end of his working day, Athena stopped him at the entrance. She held three fencing swords. Sylvano stood nearby, puzzled.

"Athena! Put those down – they're not toys, they're dangerous! What do you think you're doing?" he exclaimed.

Athena offered one of the swords to him. "I'm asking you to teach us how to fight," she said. She handed the third sword to Sylvano.

Sylvano smiled.

Father gave her a grave expression. "Wouldn't you kids rather learn a trade? Pottery, carpentry, something where nobody dies?"

"Please?" was Athena's earnest answer.

Father turned over her request in his heart. Then he took her offered sword. He hefted its weight, tested the flexibility of the blade, and regarded the reflection of his long face in its polished surface.

He stood beside his daughter and manipulated her fingers on the handle and inside the quillons of her sword. "First of all," he said, "this is the proper way to hold it. And this..." he moved her legs into a new position, "is the proper way to stand. Feet as wide apart as your shoulders, no more. Your front foot's heel in line with your back foot's toes. Never cross one leg in front of the other."

Athena smiled.

§ 9.

Athena and Sylvano faced each other in the middle of the camp's parade ground. Taller, tougher, and more sunburned than they were as children, they held out their fencing rapiers, keeping the tips in line with each other's eyes. Sylvano wore the uniform of a camp soldier and a long coat. He held a buckler, a shield the size of a dinner-plate, in his off-hand. Gripped in his fist, and held out the length of his arm, he could cover himself from another fencer at any angle. Athena's armour was second-hand, but still functional and fitting. She added several layers of quilted skirts down to her knees, a main-gauche parrying dagger in her off-hand, and a wide-brim hat to contain her curls. Seven years of gnarled fingers from kitchen-work, and the grabbing hands of soldiers, had taught her to stand tall and show strength, regardless of what she felt inside. Besides... fencing with Sylvano during her off-hours made her feel free.

"Careful Athena, that stick is sharp – you might cut yourself," Sylvano said, winking at her.

Athena brushed off his threat with a friendly snarl. "My dear Sylvano, you're making sounds out of that hole in your face again."

"Then here's a sound for you," he taunted her: "*En garde*!"

Sylvano was the first to go on the attack and lunged forward. He aimed high for Athena's face, knowing she would block it with ease, but betting he may be able to trap her blade in his buckler when she swung his sword away. But Athena stepped to one side, deflecting his attack with her rapier and blocking his buckler with her dagger at the same time. Her riposte aimed low, at his knees. He stepped out of its way but crossed his front foot in front of his back foot to do it – a mistake that Athena seized to her advantage by stepping in close enough to strike with her dagger. Sylvano had to jump to avoid losing his balance and falling to the ground. He felt the scrape of her dagger across his belly. It did not pierce his armour, but it did remind him she had trained with these weapons since both were children: she knew what she was doing.

Athena made the next advance – feinting high with the rapier, then thrusting to the middle. His buckler blocked it, but she tipped its bottom rim, allowing her to get past his defence and strike at his knees. He swerved his rapier into the defence, caught her blade in its quillons, and twisted it high. This kept her rapier out of harm's way. He arched his arm, hoping to strike at her head while keeping her rapier trapped. But Athena foresaw this move, and closed again, to trap his buckler in the quillons of her parrying dagger.

A stalemate. The only way to escape was for both to disengage. Sylvano swept his foot out to trip her and, as she stepped back to avoid the sweep, he pushed with both arms, attempting to wrestle her to the ground.

With a subtle shift in Athena's hips, they both fell but with Athena landing on top of Sylvano. He rolled with the momentum, aiming to trap her rapier under his body and perhaps capture it for himself in his off hand. To his surprise, it worked. Athena rolled to the side to keep her grip on her rapier and Sylvano saw his chance to strike with his buckler. But he found the tip of Athena's second blade poised beneath his chin, ready to thrust up and into his brain.

"*Arret*!" shouted the referee.

Both combatants froze in a tense tableau; Sylvano held his heavy blow and Athena stopped her precision-strike. Both smiled for each other, appreciating the other's effort and respecting their talent.

"First touch to Athena!" The referee declared.

Sylvano opened his hand to help Athena back to her feet, and Athena took it. They punched each other on the shoulder like siblings at play.

"Good one," said Sylvano.

"You made me earn it," Athena returned the compliment. They resumed their fighting stances for the second round of the bout.

Across the parade ground, Patroclus Crave, now a colonel and the base commander, walked behind the bench where the other fencing students sat and watched the match. A small train of officers followed him, talking among each other; but each kept one eye on their commander, in case something one of them said might catch his ear. The colonel's eyes, however, lay on the drama unfolding in the parade ground. His valet offered him his morning coffee. He took his first sip without breaking his gaze on the match.

"Who's the girl?" he asked the nearest officer.

"Her name's Athena, she's a kitchen helper," said an officer.

"Daughter of the head carpenter," said another, hoping to be helpful.

The colonel observed Athena and Sylvano at play; every thrust and parry, each feint and repost, and every scratch of steel upon steel.

"*Arret*!" The referee cried, when Sylvano struck Athena's sword-hand with his rapier and caused her to fall into his next strike. "Second touch to Sylvano! The score is even."

Athena applauded him. Sylvano wedged his toe under her sword, kicked it up, and tossed it back to her.

"And the boy?" Colonel Crave asked.

"Corporal Rizio," came the answer from another officer. "We drafted his family into the labour corps. But he joined the infantry of his own free will two years ago. He's better with muskets than with rapiers... he may actually lose this match."

"If the girl wins," Crave said to his officers, "draft her."

"I'll have the conscription papers ready before the match is done," said a third eager officer, and he dashed away to the fort's administration cabin.

Athena and Sylvano faced each other to fight for the third and winning point in the match. The audience had grown larger, and now included a few men who, Athena knew, would love nothing more than to see her lose. She could hear their taunts from the sidelines: "Put her back in her place, Rizio!", "Show us your legs, girl!"

Athena made the first move. She circling the tip of her rapier to dodge his countermoves while searching for an opening. By keeping that tip close to his eyes, her opponent remained more than a sword-length away – too far for either of them to score a point, but close enough to make hair-raising scratches of steel upon steel. The fencing rapier, her father had taught her, was made for piercing and thrusting, not for slashing. It conferred no advantage upon the heavy and the strong but it rewarded the smart and the fast. Sylvano knew that too, of course but Athena sensed that he had acquired some bad sword habits from his army training. His defence relied on his buckler more than on the fort of the sword. Athena feinted left, then struck right, and moved in to trap his sword in the quillons of her dagger before he could strike back. The gambit worked – Sylvano lost his leverage. But Athena had stepped too close and her sword-tip was past Sylvano's shoulders. She swung back to the left, so that her blade-edge could slice across his belly and score the final point. However Sylvano stepped away and knocked her sword to the side with his buckler, denying her the score.

The move had taken them both close to the edge of the parade ground. Spectators on the benches jumped out of the way. Sylvano rushed at his opponent and Athena jumped over the empty bench and kicked it to the side. Sylvano tripped upon it and fall to the ground.

The colonel, still watching, laughed.

The sound caused Sylvano's face to flush. He rolled away to avoid Athena's thrust, while swiping at her ankles with his rapier. It was a move she avoided with a skip and a hop. In the time it took him to spring back to his feet, Athena had cut off the top a banner that hung on a nearby wall, and so it fell to cover his face.

The base commander laughed louder, and more of the audience laughed with him.

Sylvano threw the banner away and lunged at Athena; the periphery of his vision red with angry blood. But Athena was ready for the move and sliced her rapier toward his wrist. The blow struck his buckler, keeping him safe, but he lost the shield in the exchange.

His balance restored, but for the echo of his fellow soldier's derisive laughter, Sylvano resolved in his heart that Athena must not be seen to win. The nearest rapier for his free hand was sheathed on the belt of another soldier, watching and mocking him from the sidelines. Sylvano swept one of his feet behind the soldier's ankle, while in the same moment giving him a gentle push on the shoulder. It was enough to make the surprised soldier step back, twist, trip, and fall giving Sylvano the split-second needed to reach around his belly from behind and steal the sword out of its scabbard.

The audience laughed at the soldier now. Sylvano apologized to him with a shrug of his shoulders and a wry smile. The soldier gave him a rude gesture in reply, though he too was smiling, admiring the audacity. Athena, for her part, tipped her hat to him.

Now armed with two blades, Sylvano rushed at his adversary again. Athena blinked at the unexpected threat, and the glint of the sun reflecting from his blades. She preserved her poise nonetheless, and flipped her dagger in her off-hand blade-up to prepare for the attack. She deflected his first blade with her rapier – the clang caused the hairs on her arms to raise. Then she twisted her shoulder out of the way to avoid his second rapier. It wasn't quite enough as the flat of his blade slapped her upper arm. She trapped Sylvano's first sword in the quillons of her own, then bent to one side, forcing Sylvano to choose between disengaging the attack or twisting his own arm out of its socket. His first blade now out of reach, she spun her sword around, releasing the trap but striking his fingers, causing him to drop the sword. Sylvano spun around almost in tandem with her, hoping to slash with his second and win the point by sheer strength and momentum. His second blade sailed safely over Athena's head as she ducked out of the way. In that moment, as he turned his back to her for a fraction of a heartbeat, he realized his mistake. He gave Athena the chance to poke his kidneys with her dagger, trip his ankles with her sword, and leave him lying on the ground with her boot on his wrist and her sword-point at his neck.

"*Arret*!" the referee called out. "Third point to Athena – and match!"

Athena released Sylvano's wrist and helped him back to his feet. Laughing, they embraced and held each other's shoulders.

"Whatever happened to letting me win if other people are watching?" Sylvano asked with a grin.

"What? There are other people watching?" Athena pretended to be surprised by the audience and the applause.

Sylvano gestured to his squad-mates, jeering and mocking him for having been bested by a girl. "Back to the kitchen with you, Rizio!" they shouted at him.

Sylvano smiled, but turned his face away, so no one would see the redness on his cheeks.

Athena saw it anyway. "Would beating me be worth anything, if I didn't give you my best?" she asked him.

Before Sylvano could answer, Colonel Crave crossed the parade ground to join them. "Well done, both of you, well done!" he congratulated them. He gestured to his orderly, who carried two small clay tankards of beer on a serving-tray. "A reward for putting on such a good show, under this hot summer sun."

Athena drank. She came to the bottom of the cup quickly and found something heavy and metallic slip down from the cup and onto her tongue. She caught it before accidentally swallowing it – a new-minted silver coin.

Before she could ask how the coin got into the beer, two officers moved to flank her, each holding their hands on their holstered pistols.

"I see you've taken the king's coin," said the colonel. "You're under my orders now."

With those words, the coin in her fingers seemed scorching hot. She flung it to the ground. "The fuck?" she protested.

The two officers grabbed her arms.

"I saw you holding in your hand a silver mark with the king's likeness, that you accepted from me freely," said the colonel.

"You hid it in the beer!" Athena shouted.

"You bested one of my soldiers in a fair fight, here on my parade," The colonel grunted. "What did you expect would happen?"

With a nod of his head, he ordered the two officers to haul Athena away.

Sylvano stepped forward. "That wasn't fair, you know."

"Nothing in life is fair," Colonel Crave replied. "Get used to it."

§ 10.

Athena struggled, swore, and fought against the officers. They marched her down the parade while a third officer held her in check with a pistol. She knew the threat was real. Having lived in the fort for seven years, she had seen unwilling recruits shot in the knees and crippled for life. Deserters, she had seen, were shot in the heart.

The officers took Athena to the camp's apothecary. The walls were lined with shelves holding bottles, phials, jars, and pots. A fireplace lay on the opposite wall from the door; the brickwork around it bore various metal portals where things could be baked or cooked at different temperatures, given the distance from the fire.

"Why are we in the alchemy lab?" Athena asked.

"For your initiation," said a man who stood by a workbench near the fireplace. He wore an officer's uniform, but unlike other officers he had shaved his head entirely bald and covered his skull with tattoos.

The officers forced Athena into the chair and tied down her ankles and wrists.

"The coin, please," the alchemist said.

"I threw it away," Athena told him.

"No matter, I have plenty more here." The alchemist rubbed an ointment on the back of Athena's right hand; it stung somewhat and smelled of rotting meat. She recoiled, but the bonds on her wrist held her fast.

"You might have noticed," said the alchemist, as he took up a coin with a pair of tweezers and doused it in a jar full of another foul-smelling substance, "that everybody around here has a coin grafted on to the back of their right hands. It's there to remind them of their loyalties."

With the officers holding her hand in position, the alchemist placed the coin on her hand. The chemicals sizzled together, and a curl of smoke rose up. Athena howled with the pain. "You goat-fucker! You might have told me it would hurt!"

"Oh, come now, we all go through this," said the alchemist. He showed her the back of his own right hand and, it too bore a coin that was grafted in place. But his was solid gold.

"I bet you *like* doing this to people, don't you!" Athena spat at him.

"The other reason we do this," the alchemist explained, as he bandaged her hand, "is in case you try to escape. Anywhere you go, people will see this coin, and they'll know to send you back to us. We pay a very generous bounty for deserters."

Athena stopped struggling against her bonds. She felt her hair crinkle and strain on her scalp. Her breath held in her throat. The dream of escaping the fort vanished with the smoke escaping out the fireplace and into the sky.

§ 11.

When Athena decided it was late enough at night, she crept out of her bed and tapped on Sylvano's shoulder to wake him up. Thirty other soldiers slept in bunk beds in the cabin – they were snoring, turning over, or covering their heads with their blankets to muffle the sound of quiet whimpering. Conscripts like herself, she knew; and all of them too terrified to escape.

"Wake up," she whispered into Sylvano's ear.

Sylvano grumbled and opened his eyes. "What is it, Kildare?"

"Want to get out of here?" she asked him.

"What... tonight?"

"I can't stay in this horrible place a single moment longer," Athena said.

"A few more days – can you give me that?" Sylvano asked.

"You've been saying that for seven years," Athena reminded him.

"But I'm a corporal now," Sylvano said. "I can get close to him. Even when I'm off-duty."

"I think you're getting to *like* it here," Athena said, annoyed.

"Nobody here knows my mother's a *strega*," Sylvano defended himself. "People treat me with respect."

"They don't treat girls with much respect, here," Athena reminded him with a grunt.

Sylvano nodded, acknowledging her truth. "One more day, then," he promised again. "Give me one more day, and the man who stole our lives will get what he deserves."

Athena took his hand and attempted to draw him out of bed. "I can't wait another day," she told him. "But I won't survive out there alone. And *you* won't survive in here... even if you succeed, they'll kill you."

"Then I'll die a free man," Sylvano hissed.

Athena leaned closer and shook her head. "But you'll still die."

Sylvano showed her the coin grafted on the back of his right hand. He pulled her hand next to his, to compare the coins. "We're dead already," he said.

§ 12.

Sylvano's commanding officer pulled him out of the breakfast lineup.

"Corporal Rizio! You're guarding the brig today," he said.

"What did I do to deserve that?" Sylvano asked.

"You lost a duel to a girl," the officer grinned in reply, and gave him a rough shove to get him moving.

The fort's prison was underground. This meant there was only one way in or out, with no possibility of breaking windows or walls to escape. The stairs led down to a tunnel, with rows of cells on each side. Three other soldiers stood in the antechamber, with pistols, daggers, and muskets at the ready.

"Tight security today," Sylvano observed.

"Have you ever seen a fringer?" Colonel Crave asked him. "Up close, that is?"

"No, never," Sylvano said.

The officer nodded to the other soldiers. "Bring out our honoured guest."

They opened one of the cells and marched its shackled occupant into the corridor. At first, Sylvano thought the prisoner was a man perhaps a few years older than himself. But as the prisoner entered the lamplight of the guard station, he could see the differences. His arms and legs were strong but tired – like a blacksmith's forge whose fire had gone out. His fingers were long, and his ears tapered to points. His flesh was dark purple in tone and lacked all hair of any kind. What caused Sylvano to tense with surprise, however, was the golden glow emanating from his eyes. It resembled two dim candles in the darkened corridor. In another place and under better light, he may have been a proud king on a sacred throne. But here in the camp's prison, he was a mere man... tired, fearful, and sad. The soldiers pushed him into a chair and fastened his shackles to it.

"This *creature*, sitting here before you, is an *astron*," Colonel Crave explained. "They come from the Scatterlands. Or maybe somewhere beyond. Doesn't matter. What *does* matter is that they don't belong here, in Summerland." He loaded and primed a wheel-lock pistol and handed it to Sylvano. "Kill it," he ordered.

The *astron* gazed up at Sylvano with a look that reminded him of all the times other children in his village taunted and spat at him, calling him the son of a *strega* – the son of a witch. Here was someone he could spit on and who might himself be the offspring of witches. It was someone his officer gave him permission to abuse. He took the weapon and unlocked its safety catch. He took aim and then he held the weapon steady, without moving.

"You want to get your honour back after losing to a girl in front of the whole camp? Kill the prisoner!" The commander taunted him.

Upstairs, the soldier posted at the prison's entrance jumped at the sudden stroke of gunfire from the tunnel.

§ 13.

Sylvano crept across the floor of the barracks, with only the moonlight through the windows to show him the way. He tapped Athena on the shoulder.

"You were right, Athena," he whispered to her.

"Sylvano? Right about what?" she mumbled back, as she turned over in her bed to face him.

"We have to get out of here," he answered. "As soon as we can."

Athena roused herself to full wakefulness in a heartbeat. She threw off her blankets, revealing she was still fully dressed.

"Let's go," she said.

They stole across the fort whenever the clouds covered the two moons. The pair were moving under carts, behind barrels, and beneath the catwalks on the ramparts.

"Athena... isn't the way out toward the *edge* of the camp, not the centre?" Sylvano asked, as they skirted the side of the officer's cabin.

"I made survival packs for us today," she told him. "I hid them in the garden outside the colonel's bedroom."

"He's the *last* person we want to wake up tonight!" Sylvano said, alarmed.

"It's also the last place anyone would look," Athena reminded him with a grin.

They waited for the clouds to dim the light and chose their moment to creep into the shrubbery beneath the commander's window.

"You made these today?" Sylvano asked. "But, how did you know I would want to leave tonight?"

"Yes, how *did* I know you'd want to go tonight?" Athena said, grinning. "Such a mystery! Almost as if I've known you for the whole of your life."

Sylvano grinned and carried on.

Careful that their footsteps fell no louder than the crickets and night peepers, the two deserters collected the packs Athena had made, and retreated to the safety of a nearby stack of crates. The fort offered very few hiding places; it was designed so that most of its area could be seen from the watch towers and attacked from those towers if the walls were ever breached. Sentries sat on those towers, some with three or four muskets primed and ready so that they need not waste time reloading in a fight. Athena and Sylvano could count on them facing the wilderness outside, and not the grounds within but they knew that would change if they made any suspicious noises.

"I had a chance, today," Sylvano said. "But I didn't take it."

"A chance to – to do it?" Athena asked.

"He was as near to me as you are now," Sylvano told the story. "Handed me his own pistol. Only two other guards in the room. I could have... could have shot him and ran."

"You wouldn't have got far," Athena said.

Sylvano shrugged. "But that's not the reason I didn't do it," he said. "I've been thinking of nothing else all day. I've been thinking..."

Sylvano took in the scene around him: the night clouds, the silhouette of the sentry towers and the treeline beyond, and the drifting scent of campfire smoke. He scuttled backward, making himself small at the approaching footsteps of a pair of soldiers on the path. When they passed, he saw they were too drunk to notice him.

"Before we go," Sylvano said, "there's someone else who needs to get out of here. I owe it to him, to help him."

"All the other kids from our village got taken to other camps," Athena reminded him.

"This one's a friend I met this morning," Sylvano said.

Stealing from one shadow to another, he led her to the entrance to the prison.

"We can't break anyone out of there," Athena complained.

"There's only one prisoner down there right now," said Sylvano. "And he didn't do anything to deserve it. We have to help him, if we can."

"I only made two survival kits," Athena informed him.

"If we don't break him out, he will die," Sylvano said. His voice caused a stir in a nearby tent. The two deserters ducked behind another tent, and kept their heads low until the witness to their noise closed the tent again and went back to sleep.

"So, who is he?" Athena asked.

"I don't actually know his name," said Sylvano. "Never mind, come on!"

Sylvano ducked inside the prison door, careful to keep it as narrow and quiet as possible.

"You *had* to make it more complicated," Athena complained, as though Sylvano could still hear him. Then she followed him inside.

In the antechamber, two soldiers sat at a table, playing a card game. They rose when Sylvano and Athena entered.

"We're here to relieve you," said Sylvano.

"A bit early for a shift change," said one of the guards. "And why aren't you in uniform?"

"We're here to relieve you in a different sense of the word," Sylvano replied. And before the guards could respond, Sylvano clubbed him on the head with his own bottle of wine. He fell back into his chair, surrounded by shards of glass.

The second guard reached for his pistol. But before he could grasp it, Athena took a sword from a nearby rack and snapped its sharp tip across the soldier's fingers. The guard next reached for the rope that rang the alarm bell but Sylvano kicked the table in front of him, knocking him to the ground. Athena finished the job by bludgeoning him into unconsciousness with the pommel of her sword.

"We weren't here for one of these two idiots, were we?" Athena asked.

"No. We're here for *him*," said Sylvano, gesturing toward the row of cells. Taking the guard's keys, he unlocked one of them.

A figure in shadow stirred at the sight of the opened door. Two candles appeared in the dark – his eyes... opening.

"Hey! You awake in there? Would you care for more comfortable accommodations?" Sylvano asked.

The figure sat up from the wooden bench that served as his bed, but did not speak. The clanking and rattling of his shackles did his speaking for him.

Sylvano held up the ring of keys. The prisoner rose and dragged his chains to the cell door.

"Why?" he asked. His voice was low and exhausted.

"I'll tell you when we're safely far away," Sylvano promised. He released the *astron* from the shackles.

The former prisoner examined his wrists as if he had never seen them before. "I could kill you with my bare hands, for what you did today," he said.

Athena perked an eyebrow, wondering what Sylvano did.

"Let's save *that* for later too," Sylvano said.

As Sylvano and Athena dragged one guard by his wrists and ankles, the *astron* took the other guard under one of his arms. He noticed Athena staring at him.

"Who are you?" he asked.

"I'm – I'm nobody," Athena stammered.

Sylvano stepped between them. "We don't have time, friends," he reminded them.

They clapped the shackles on the guards and locked the door.

"Now, Athena, you were saying something about a hole in the outer wall?" said Sylvano.

"He's too big to fit through," Athena said, nodding toward the *astron*. "But I have another idea."

After some scavenging and scrounging about the camp, Athena and Sylvano pushed a cart along the path to the nearest gate, with the *astron* lying under a blanket on the cart. Sylvano approached the sentries on duty there. "Open the gate," Sylvano asked him.

"By whose order?" said a sentry.

"This man's, right here," said Sylvano, showing the *astron's* purple foot from under the blanket. "Half an hour ago, he just barfed up everything he ever ate in his life and died. Who knew the fringers could do that? We're taking him out to bury him."

The sentry stepped near, to take a closer look. "Is that the thing we captured last week?" he asked.

Athena covered their friend's foot again. "You don't want to get too close," she said. "In case he died of something catching!"

"All right, all right," the sentry agreed. He waved to his companions; they unbarred the gate and opened it.

"Back in about an hour," said Sylvano, smiling.

The three escapees got less than twenty paces from the gate when the sentry jogged up to them. "Excuse me," he said. "If you're going out to bury a body, why don't you have any shovels with you?"

Sylvano and Athena exchanged anguished looks. Silently, each accused the other of forgetting the shovels.

"Yeah, if you wouldn't mind going back to the camp and getting them for us?" Sylvano asked.

The sentry clapped his hand down on the cart. "I think I'll wake up the colonel instead."

The *astron* threw off the blanket and grabbed the sentry by his collar.

An inarticulate gurgle of horror spilled up from the sentry's throat. The former prisoner then pointed two fingers of his free hand at the sentry's face and closed one eye.

"Your life will *change*," he intoned, his voice deep and guttural. Then he threw the sentry to the ground.

The sentry scuttled away, wild-eyed and shaking. He put his thumb between his middle two fingers and drew a circle in the air – a gesture of warding against curses. "Ar'vanor, the Father of Men, my shield and my protector..." he prayed.

Athena and Sylvano looked at each other and almost laughed, amazed that the former prisoner's power was on their side.

The other sentry ran back to the camp, shouting to wake the other soldiers: "The prisoner's escaped, the prisoner escaped!"

The *astron* looked askance at his rescuers. "What are you waiting for? Run!" he told them.

They ran into the forest. With the two moons emerged from the clouds, there was light enough to see the path, but not quite enough to see the tree roots or stones strewn across it. Each of them tripped and stumbled more than once or scrambled to stay on their feet. They were not quite out of range of the camp's guns when they heard the trumpets and bells rousing the soldiers from their barracks, and the shouts of officers organizing a search.

Athena veered off the path and into thicker cover, in the hope the sentries might not want to follow. Low hanging branches whipped her face and arms; the shadows made them too dark to see. Her footsteps in the leaf-litter and the twigs made almost as much noise as her backpack. She found a hollow in the lee of a small rock-stack and crouched down in it. She primed her wheel-lock, ready if she needed it.

The shouting of the sentries came from more directions. Athena surmised they were fanning out, searching for them. A shadow loomed near – a sentry, less than a stone's throw away.

Athena balanced her pistol-arm on her knee, to steady her aim, but another thought occurred to her. Reaching with her free hand, she retrieved from under her brocade the wooden figurine of the winged rabbit, which hung on a string around her neck. She grasped it in her fist and pressed it to her heart. She worked out in her mind whether she was alone enough to use it, and whether the danger was enough to need the second of only two remaining lifelines. If she called for Dubhdarra now, would he come soon enough? And who knows whether in twenty years she might be in a worse fix, but she had used all three of her lifelines?

The sentry moved slowly, careful of the noise his feet made in the underbrush, with his musket ready to fire. His head darted around, glancing left and right and left again, as though he feared for his life as much as Athena feared for her own. He was facing not quite away from her, but not quite toward her – the smallest twitch of her toe might still attract his attention. Athena wrapped herself in stillness and silence; she willed herself not to flinch when a spider climbed up her arm.

A flurry of leaves, and a trembling of branches, and then a moving shadow – the *astron* came around the rock-stack from the other side and crouched down. He was quieter than Athena had been. Perhaps the forest knew him and muffled his steps to protect him. But in the place he chose to hide, the soldier was sure to soon find the glowing of his golden eyes in the blue-black night.

"You might as well come out... we'll burn down the forest to find you!" shouted the soldier.

And Athena realized that neither of them knew she was there. She could save the *astron's* life, though she had never met him before and owed nothing to him. Or perhaps she did owe him something, as any self-aware being owes it to another to come to their aid when their life is in peril. She took aim at the sentry with her pistol. If she fired, Athena knew the sound would alert all the sentries to her presence, and they would return fire without hesitation.

And if she fired and hit, then she will have killed a man. She had never killed a man before.

What was more, she knew the soldier's name. She had served him breakfast and dinner in the canteen for seven years.

He shouted for his companions but Athena heard no further footsteps in the undergrowth of the forest... only the toads and crickets, and the creaking of branches in the wind. The clouds covered one of the moons, darkening the world again. No other sentries were close enough to answer his call. The *astron* made a tentative step away, keeping his eyes low and half-covered with his hand – the sentry heard the crack of a twig underfoot. He primed the wheel of his pistol, and was ready and prepared to kill.

Athena lined up her sights, steadied her arm on her knee, closed her eyes, and fired.

When she opened her eyes again, the sentry lay on the ground. The *astron* stood near him, glancing about, searching for his saviour.

"Over here," Athena whispered.

The *astron* nodded and looted the sentry's weapons, boots, and coat. He then joined Athena in the protection of the rock-stack. "Is the other human with you?" he whispered.

"No, it's just me," she said.

The *astron* made himself comfortable on the ground and touched the soil with his long fingers. "The river protects him. We need only wait for the sentries to realize this," he said.

"How do you know?" Athena asked.

"Quiet," the *astron* warned her. "Or they'll hear you."

They crept across the forest floor, to a window in the treeline, careful to avoid making noise or being seen. They saw the soldiers advancing their line across a tall-grass meadow that sloped down toward a riverbank. Reaching the edge, their leader tested the water.

"The current's too strong to cross," he told his squad. "And the nearest bridge is three leagues from here. They have to be somewhere along the banks. Fan out and find them!"

The squad fanned out with half going upriver and the other half going down.

When the soldiers were out of earshot, the *astron* let out a long breath, and let his shoulders relax. "What's your name, young human?" he asked as he sat up.

"Athena," she said. "Athena Kildare."

"A queenly name, in more than one language," he said. Touching his breast, he said, "Wicklow. And thank you, for saving my life."

Athena pursed her lips. "I had to kill a man to do it," she said, looking down.

Wicklow perked his brow. "A curious complaint, from a soldier," he said.

"They press-ganged me yesterday," Athena grunted. "It's why I had to escape."

They came to the riverbank. Its water was fast-moving, just as the sentry leader had said, and its depths seemed black and bottomless even as the light of the two moons brightened it.

Wicklow stepped into the shallows. The waves lapped no higher on him than the tops of his toes. It bore him over its surface as though he walked on solid earth – Athena gasped, then made an awkward laugh.

"What's so funny?" Wicklow asked her.

"They told us the only magic fringers can do is curse people," Athena replied.

"I don't have the dark magic," he said. "But that sentry doesn't know that, does he?" The shape of a grin grew on the side of his face, for the first time.

Athena grasped the implications and laughed.

§ 14.

"Who knew that *astrons* could do that, eh Athena?" Sylvano exclaimed, delighted to see them as they found each other again.

Wicklow only glanced at him, letting Sylvano believe whatever he wanted about what more and what else he could do.

"We should keep moving," he said. "At least until morning. I know a place where we can camp for the night."

They walked in silence for a while, though Athena sensed the tension rising in Sylvano.

"In my defence – I had to do it," Sylvano blurted out, when he could no longer hold back. "They'd have shot *me* if I refused."

"We all do what we have to do," Wicklow said. "That's the oldest story we tell ourselves, isn't it?"

Athena said, "Will one of you tell me what you're talking about?"

Wicklow regarded Sylvano, expecting the truth from him, but prepared for the lie.

Sylvano took a breath, and said, "I did something I knew to be wrong. But I did it anyway."

Wicklow gestured to invite Sylvano to continue.

"They posted me to guard the brig," Sylvano said. "The colonel handed me a pistol and told me to kill the – to kill Wicklow. I took the weapon, and I shot him. Didn't even think about it."

Athena, puzzled, said, "Then how is it he's not dead?"

Wicklow supplied the answer. "Because they loaded the pistol with blanks," he said. "They didn't want to kill me; I'm too valuable to them. They wanted to test his obedience."

Athena took a moment to comprehend the story. "Lucky then, that you didn't take your chance on the colonel himself," she said.

Sylvano shook his head. "Seven years of thinking about revenge... thinking about almost nothing else. Seven years of following orders, too. So, when the chance for revenge was in my hands, what did I do instead? I followed orders. And now all I can think about is: what happened to me? Am I turning into the colonel? Who am I, now?"

Athena placed a caring hand on his shoulder.

Wicklow said, "For the moment, you're an outlaw. Athena, so are you. No one will show us any kindness unless they *want* something from us. I've lived all my life in places where I don't belong... I can tell you all about that."

"Is that how you ended up in the brig?" asked Athena.

"Your army wanted me to work for them," the *astron* said. "But they wanted too much, and didn't pay enough. So, I refused. They raided my camp. In truth, I think they didn't *need* a reason to raid us. I think they did it for fun."

The trio came to a clearing in the forest, by the side of an overgrown dirt road. The charred and blackened remains of several wagons, caravans, and jaunting carts lay strewn across the dry ground. Wicklow wandered about the ruin, smelling the acrid air. Then he sat on the ground and suppressed his tears.

"I'm going to Dawnland, to find the Gates of the Morning," Athena said to him.

Wicklow gave her a puzzled, patronizing look.

"She's serious," Sylvano told Wicklow. "The whole fort had to listen to her talk about it for years."

"But I *am* serious," Athena insisted. Remembering something Dubhdarra once told her, she added, "And I want you both to come with me."

Sylvano shook his head. "You're crazy, Athena!" he laughed. "Crazier than my mother, and she didn't know her own face in a mirror. The Gates of the Morning – they're an old sailor's tale. They don't exist."

But Wicklow spoke in a tone that suggested he believed her. "Are you so sure?" he replied to Sylvano.

"Why... have you been there? Seen them for yourself?"

"I've been to the Scatterlands," Wicklow reported with pride. "Many times."

"Then your answer to my question is *no*," Sylvano concluded with a smirk. "So why don't we go up north, to the mountains? Nothing but mining towns and logging tows up there. Easy to hide, from the army."

Athena chose her moment to enter the fray. "You're afraid, aren't you Sylvano?" she asked, grinning.

"No," Sylvano said, without hesitating. Then he added, "I just... I think that... Even if the Gates of the Morning *do* exist – and I'm not saying they do – how could we even find it?"

"You employ the services of a Navigator," said Wicklow. "And in case you're wondering how to find one – you already have."

Athena saw her new friend in a new light. She leaned toward him. "You know the way to Dawnland?" she said. Excitement grew in her face.

"I'll take you as far as Port Vivaldi, first," Wicklow promised. "That much, I think I owe you. But if you want to go to Dawnland, you'll need a ship, and you'll need to pay my fee."

Sylvano shrugged and opened his hands. "And we can't afford that. Obviously. So, how about this for a plan… We go up north, and then we shake hands and go our separate ways."

"That's not a plan," Athena complained. "That's like, the complete *opposite* of a plan."

"Still better than your plan," Sylvano shot back. "Because you don't have one."

"Yes, I do," Athena said. "We follow the Whisperlights."

"The… what?" Sylvano asked.

The *astron* looked up, astonished. "You've never heard of the Whisperlights? Did you grow up locked in a garret?" he said.

"We grew up in the camp," Sylvano said.

Wicklow grasped this and showed more compassion in his demeanour.

"I saw them, once," said Athena. "Like fireflies, but with more colours, and… it was like they could *talk* if they wanted to. Like they *knew* me."

Wicklow nodded. "When you see them from a distance, they look like magic," he said. "But when you walk among them, they're parasites. They get into your head. They'll make you feel worthless, unwanted, unlovable. You're living the worst day of your life, all over again. I think they *feed* on those feelings. And when they let you go, you'll find you were gone for *days*. Some people…" he paused for a moment, looking away, "some never come back at all."

Athena tried to reconcile Wicklow's report with what Dubhdarra had advised her. Dubhdarra was one of the few people in her life who had treated her with unconditional kindness, and who asked nothing from her in return. But it was clear to her that Wicklow spoke from experience.

Sylvano broke the silence. "Looks like all we can do is find somewhere to hide. Somewhere we can put our heads back on straight. And I like the mountains. Always wanted to climb one."

But Athena was resolute. "Climb any mountain you want, and it won't be high enough. As long as we wear the tags," she pointed to the coin on the back of her hand. "It's only a matter of time before someone turns us in, for the bounty. But, if we go to the Scatterlands, nobody will follow us. And maybe the gods can answer your question."

Sylvano pursed his lips, disliking her argument, or perhaps disliking the fact that Athena might be right.

"And you, Wicklow," Athena continued, "Yes, I've heard stories of people getting lost in the Whisperlights. But I can't believe it's worse than having your camp burned down, and you yourself locked in a dungeon."

Wicklow looked to the ground and stirred some ashes with a stick.

"So you've lost your people," Athena continued. "And I'm sorry. But maybe the *astrons* have a homeland, somewhere out there. Maybe you have more people than you know. And maybe the gods can tell you where they are."

Wicklow stirred the ground with his stick again. He made a long, sorrowful sigh. "Will you help me to bury my friends, before we go?" he asked.

Athena nodded and closed her eyes. "Of course I will," she agreed.

They found some tools in a caravan that had been spared most of the fire. It lay on its side at the edge of the clearing. Sylvano paced back and forth around the site, sometimes gazing down the road at the life that lay ahead of him: a life whose shape he could not yet see.

"Sylvano?" Athena prodded him.

Sylvano nodded. "All right, I'm coming too," he said. He found a pickaxe under a pile of broken wagon parts and helped his companions to dig.

In the darkness between the trees that surrounded them, the Whisperlights gathered to watch. Seeing them there, few and dim yet clear and alive, Athena decided she had found the friends she needed to bring with her to Dawnland.

Dubhdarra, watching from a distance, smiled to see her happy.

§ 15.

They salvaged all the clothing, tools, and money that they could find from the remains of the traveller camp. Athena and Sylvano found some mismatched gloves to cover the coins grafted on their hands and Wicklow covered his bare head with a turban.

"We should follow the hedgerows and the deer trails," Wicklow advised as they set out for the city. "The roads will not be safe for us."

They ate whatever they could steal from travellers' hostels and farmhouses, and camped in empty barns and in gullies where they could light a small cooking fire unseen. They took turns keeping watch while others slept, but Athena lay awake during Wicklow's turn. She kept a dagger hidden beneath her bedroll, near to her hand.

"You don't trust him," Sylvano said, one day while they walked together out of Wicklow's earshot.

"Do you?" she asked in return.

"Doesn't matter whether I trust him – we need him," Sylvano answered. "He knows the way."

"I know we need him… that's why I asked him to come," Athena said.

"But you don't trust him," Sylvano repeated.

Athena gave herself a moment to craft her answer. "I do trust him. But I wonder what he's not telling us. He's afraid of something."

They followed Wicklow through fields of corn, lettuce, and potatoes, through pastures, and through thick forests where woodcutters and charcoal-burners made their camps. At the crest of a hill, Wicklow suggested that they rest near a window in the trees that opened to the full scope of the world. Beyond which were wide and deep valleys, the glistening ponds, the subtle aroma of new-planted fields, and warm sun on their arms and faces. The swift-moving clouds cast their shadows over the land, turning all the world into a glorious rolling sea of greens, hues of gold, and reveries.

Seeing Athena held in awe, Wicklow said, "That's why we call it Summerland."

In the far distance to the south, Athena could see a band of deep blue on the horizon and feel a warm humid wind coming from it. "Is that the ocean?" she asked.

"The Heartwater," Wicklow named it. "An inland sea. The ocean is another five hundred leagues further east. You were wondering what I'm afraid of? It's that the two of you don't know anything about the world we live in."

Athena and Sylvano traded sheepish gestures, realizing Wicklow could hear them all along, and admitting that he was right.

"And I assume you've never seen a *city*, either?" Wicklow asked them, as he walked further on.

"Never," said Athena.

Wicklow said, "Then I'm sorry that your first city had to be *this* one."

Second Light: Port Vivaldi

§ 16.

Port Vivaldi lay on a score of islands in the mouth of a river that poured into the Heartwater, near its easternmost end. Though the sun had just set, the city's canals and waterways remained busy with traffic. Ferries, galleons, schooners, and yachts all tacked and paddled around each other in a kind of slow-moving chaos. The towers, palaces, and temples of the city appeared in an early evening silhouette, against a backdrop of a cherry-red sky, and the white-capped Windward Mountains in the distant north-west. Yet the city also glowed with lanterns, torches, and candles, some that hung from ropes that spanned the canals, others from the ends of long poles that reached out from the corners of the buildings. The closer Athena's ferry came to its berth, the more the city appeared to her like it floated; its stones and bricks were somehow lighter than water. The golden glow of the lamps played out across the waves as hundreds of narrow golden paths shimmering toward her, welcoming her.

Drawing closer, the boat traffic became thicker as each pilot was jostling for a better berth, or striving ahead to enter a canal before everyone else. The ferry's captain seemed familiar with the play. With a combination of cheerful greetings, rough shouting, and a few bumps against other ferries, he brought the boat to a dock with room enough for every passenger and their bags to disembark without delay. The captain advised them all of local inns and taverns where they might find food and drink, and a bed for the night. Athena didn't hear him – she was too busy gasping at the height of the towers, the elegance of their ornaments, the mosaic patterns in the cobblestones, and the sheer density of people rushing by.

A great shadow loomed over the buildings. It was long, pointed at one end, square on the other, and rumbling with a low drone. A swift breeze tangled Athena's hair.

"It's a sky-ship," Wicklow explained. "We're going to need one if we're going to Dawnland."

Athena laughed to see it.

"What's so funny?" Wicklow asked.

"Who knew the world had such audacious things in it?" she said, delighted.

The sky-ship approached one of the city's towers, and a drawbridge lowered from the tower's pinnacle to receive it. Ambient light from below revealed the ship's three long rows of gunports, its stained-glass windows in the aft-castle, and the gentle rippling of its sails.

Wicklow urged his two companions along the cobbles and toward the main market square for the island. "Keep moving, or you'll lose your purses to thieves," he said. "If not your heads."

Some hundred paces along the street, they passed by a tall and narrow building of yellow plaster and white stone framing. The wooden sign hanging over the door was painted with an image of a horse-drawn wagon under two crescent moons. Most of the passengers from the ferry went straight there from the dock.

"What's this place?" Athena asked Wicklow.

"It's a traveller's hostel," the *astron* explained. "Twenty beds to a room, but they're the cheapest beds in the city. If you're looking for a ship, this is where you might meet the crew."

Sylvano said, "Looks like we found where we're staying tonight. Meet you here after midnight, then." He walked away, his arms outstretched, looking up to the rooftops and turning in a circle as he moved.

"Where are you going?" Athena shouted after him.

"First night in the big city? After years locked up in the camp? I'm going to re-invent myself," he replied. With that, he spun round in another circle and allowed himself to be swallowed by the crowd.

Sylvano caught a snatch of familiar music from somewhere over the clamour and din of the street. It was a light-hearted, loud-belted soldier's song, on a score of young men's voices – it told of the strength and cleverness of Port Vivaldi's warriors, and the foolishness of their enemies.

He followed the sound to a tavern in a market square and stepped inside.

In the light of dozens of oil lamps that hung from chains in the ceiling, he found a room full of loud-singing, loud-living people. Nearly all of them wore a long leather jerkin with a shoulder-sash of yellow cloth. Most were armed with daggers or pistols. The arm wrestling, swearing, drinking, and boasting made Sylvano feel at home.

"A pint of your finest, please," Sylvano asked a serving-boy. He placed a few coins in the boy's hand. The boy gave Sylvano a strained look, then went to fetch the meal.

The boy tapped the arm of a soldier to draw his attention. Sylvano gathered by the soldier's embossed leather pauldrons and oiled goatee that he was probably their leader. He moved to stand by Sylvano's table, and grinned.

"Well met, friend," he said. "You look like a young man in search of adventure. What's your name?"

"Dante. Dante Carpinetto," said Sylvano, grinning, reinventing himself with a tip of his hat.

"Carpinetto – I think we have twenty bottles of that behind the bar," the man laughed.

Sylvano felt the only thing to do was laugh with him. "I'll buy you one, if you like," he offered.

The man sat down. "I'm Lieutenant Etienne d'Orsonnes", said the soldier, introducing himself. "And these associates of mine with the fashionable gold sashes are the are the men of the Volscragg Gentlemen's Society. The finest soldiers of fortune in all Summerland. *Your* fortune, too, if you sign up with us."

Sylvano grinned but tilted his head down. "A generous offer. But at this particular moment, all I'm looking for is a plate of meat, some bread and wine, and maybe someone who can point me to the residence of one Colonel Patroclus Crave. I know he has a palazzo in the city."

"Sounds like a spineless toff who powders his hair," said Etienne. "You're not looking to sign up with *him*, are you?"

"No, by the gods, no," Sylvano said. "I'm here because – I've a message for him. That's my trade. I'm a messenger."

Etienne seemed unimpressed. "You should sign up with us, instead. With us, you remain your own master. You take orders from no one, unless you choose to. And I'll tell you something else about us... we pay better."

"I've no doubt that you do," Sylvano said, still smiling. "Look, I did not realize this pub was only for gentlemen like yourself, and not for country boys like me. I apologize for troubling you. I'll be on my way."

"You know where to find us if you change your mind," said Etienne, rising from his seat. He extended his right hand, to shake. "Pleasure to meet you, mister Carpinetto."

Sylvano almost took the captain's hand but withdrew. It occurred to him that the captain wanted to know if a coin was grafted on the back of his hand.

Etienne made an expectant gesture. "You're new to our fair city, aren't you?" he said. "One of our local customs is to remove our gloves when we shake hands. Keeping them on is considered very ungentlemanly."

Now Sylvano felt he knew for certain the captain believed he was a deserter. "I'll just – I'll be going now, if that's all right," he said.

The captain drew his rapier and held it to Sylvano's heart. "What – after insulting me like that?"

Sylvano glowered at him. "You're challenging me to a *duel* for not shaking your hand?"

"Did I say 'duel'?" Etienne laughed. "Did anyone in this room hear me utter the word 'duel'?" This young country clod here has challenged me to a duel!" His audience laughed with him. But the point of his rapier remained over Sylvano's heart.

"And I accept," said the lieutenant.

With those words, the other soldiers in the room pushed the tables and benches away, making space on the floor.

Sylvano made a quick glance around the room, counting obstacles, exits, and anything that someone could use as a weapon. Though only Etienne held a sword at the ready, more than a dozen other 'gentlemen' carried swords on their belts and would raise them in a heartbeat at their leader's command. So far as Sylvano could see, there was no other way out of the tavern, but to draw his sword. It would be his first duel with someone who was not a fellow trainee from the camp. His jaw quivered and his eyes widened. Some of the other soldiers in the tavern sensed his trepidation and snickered at him.

Sylvano made the first move. He thrust to the middle, to test his opponent's reflexes. The soldier batted it aside easily, as Sylvano expected. Sylvano twisted and thrust to the middle again, this time quicker. The soldier parried it with ease again. A third testing thrust, and the soldier caught the blade in his quillons and trapped him. Sylvano withdrew to escape but tripped on a stool lying on its side on the floor behind him.

His audience laughed at him but something in Sylvano's mind doubted that the stool was there when the duel began.

Sylvano launched himself into a proper forceful attack, thrusting and sweeping with all the speed and momentum he could bring. The soldier, baffled for a moment, stepped back to avoid him. Sylvano seized the initiative to press forward some more, but had to hop to the side to avoid a chair that someone kicked on to the floor in front of him. He kept his balance, but at the cost of receiving the soldier's sword-point on his breast for the first time. Though it did not penetrate the leather of his armour, still he felt the sting of it. And equally as hurtful was the sting of the laughter from the observers, enjoying the sight of his frustration.

The two threw themselves at each other, trading presses and retreats, while trading glancing touches on shoulders, legs, and arms. Each time Sylvano found an opening or an advantage, someone in the room would throw an obstacle or a distraction before him – a puddle of wine spilled onto the floor, a handful of ashes from the fireplace, tossed near his face, or a slop bucket rolled out in front of him. Sylvano felt his focus slipping turning this into a dangerous situation; a fencer who attacks in anger always leaves an opening for the opponent.

Sylvano pressed forward, choosing the thrusts that would require his enemy to move back to parry them. This new strategy paid off – the bully retreated, and almost fell on to a bench. The beat he needed to get on his feet again was enough time for Sylvano to jump on a bench and slash at one of the lanterns that hung from the ceiling. It crashed to the floor, spilling lamp-oil in a puddle and setting it on fire. Surprised, the bully jumped back again. This too gave Sylvano the chance to dash from one table-top to another, avoiding the flames, and catching his opponent with his back facing him. Sylvano pushed the point of his blade between the bully's shoulder-blades, not enough to draw blood, but enough to show him he was beaten.

In the same instant, three soldiers drew swords and pressed them into Sylvano's back. "Drop it, kid," one of them ordered.

Sylvano read the room again. He held the captain, but with three men holding him, he had few options. He tested his luck with a careful side-step toward a wall. The three men on his back followed. Two more stepped between him and the door and lay their hands on the hilts of their pistols.

But Sylvano saw at least one exit that the Volscragg Gentlemen forgot to cover – the window. He leapt over a table and escaped the pub by crashing through the glass.

The other soldiers poured out of the pub, swords drawn, looking for their quarry. "The bounty on that one is mine!" Etienne shouted, as he joined them.

Sylvano ran.

§ 17.

"Does he always do that?" Wicklow asked Athena. "Run away by himself when he doesn't know where he's going?"

"No, this is a first, for him," Athena said.

"Well. Lucky for him, people will think he belongs here," Wicklow said, with a note of wistfulness. "You and I… we should get off the street as soon as we can."

Athena saw the evidence of this in the way many men looked at her as they passed near her, grinning with something like hunger.

"Lead the way," Athena said.

They quick-stepped along the mosaic cobblestone streets. Rounding a bend in the street, Athena slowed to admire an intricate astronomical clock on a stone watchtower that overlooked a bridge, but Wicklow tugged her elbow to keep her moving. "You have to pretend this is nothing to you, or else everyone will know you're a tourist," he said.

But a second sight caught Athena's attention – an elegant young lady sitting at a table by an outdoor café, sipping a glass of wine. She dressed in far finer clothes than Athena's: a crushed velvet brocade skirt with several petticoats beneath, a silk bodice with a frilled neckline, and a laced velvet brocade bustier. Her hat was wreathed with flowers and topped with a tall red feather. Athena imagined that the outfit might cost more money than had ever passed through her hands in her whole life. The item which caught Athena's attention the most was a silver necklace, from which hung an enamelled portrait medallion with the image of a winged rabbit.

"Eyes ahead, Athena," Wicklow reminded her.

"There's someone here I have to meet," Athena said. She stepped among the tables of the café, oblivious to the judgmental sniffs from the well-heeled café patrons.

"Pardon me," Athena said to the woman, "This might be a strange question... do you know a man named Dubhdarra Muirthemney?"

The woman glanced about the café, as though assessing who might be close enough to overhear the conversation. "I assume Vittorio sent you?" she asked, touching the witch-rabbit medallion.

"Who?" Athena asked.

"So, it was Martello, then," said the woman, holding up her medallion to admire it. "You're not the first person he sent to make me an offer on his behalf. But I've already told him why I can't part with it. Certainly not for the price he's quoting. I know you're only doing what you're told, and I'm sure he paid you well, but if you don't mind, I'm waiting to meet someone. Please give Martello my regards. I'll be happy to visit him if he ever finds himself in jail again."

"I don't know any of those people," Athena said. "The man I'm thinking of is a ranger, and..." and taking care that only Wicklow and the woman could see it, Athena produced the wooden witch-rabbit figurine for both of them to see, "he gave me this."

The woman, seeing it, dropped her jaw. She reached to touch it, though with care, as though the sight of it was a religious experience. "You met him?" she asked.

"Twice, yes," Athena said, grinning.

"Woollen cloak, walking stick, and scarf?" the woman asked.

"Talking to animals, like they understood him," Athena added, smiling, grasping that they were indeed speaking of the same person.

"Feeding them?" said the woman, sharing Athena's smile.

"Right out of his hands," Athena confirmed.

Without warning nor permission, the woman grasped Athena by the shoulders and hugged her.

Wicklow made an uncomfortable face, as the scene gathered the attention of the café patrons.

"My name's Layla," said the woman, letting Athena go. "Layla Darvi. Of the Poet's Lake Darvis. Not to be confused with the Ranger's Lake Darvis. Poet's Lake – the weather there is absolutely savage in the winter. Have you ever been?"

"I have," said Wicklow.

"Then you *know*," said Layla. She summoned the waiter with a wave of her finger. "Tea and cakes for my two guests, on my tab," she told him. "Oh, but we were just talking about Poet's Lake. Unbearable weather. Simply unbearable. So glad to be here in Port-a-vee, I can tell you."

"You were waiting for someone?" Wicklow asked, looking for a reason to leave.

"*You*, I think," Layla said, speaking low again, and still smiling. "Dubhdarra told me that some day I would meet someone who also carried his token, and that – well, never mind me. My story's not important. What about you? What brings you to our fair city? Have you seen the new opera house yet? They just finished building it. The grand staircase has the most wonderful lampposts... solid redwood imported all the way from Darkenland. You must see it before you do anything else! And – how long will you be here? You're not staying at one of the traveller's hostels by the ferry docks, I hope. They're not safe. Most of those sailors haven't seen a woman in months – you ken me? So, you *must* stay with me tonight. I insist. Both of you."

"We would be delighted to stay with you for the night," said Athena, with cheer.

"No, we would not," Wicklow said, not caring that Layla could hear. She leaned toward Athena and said, "Can I talk to you for a moment?"

Layla gave them both a knowing smirk.

"It's all right, Wicklow, we can trust her," Athena promised.

"How can you be sure?" the faeborn replied. "And who is this 'Dubhdarra'? Did you break me out of one camp only to lock me to another?"

"No, I promise you, no," said Layla. "Dubhdarra's a kind of traveller. Or actually... that's not quite right. More like the kind of old friend who you don't see very often, but when you do, it's like he never left. When did you first meet him? Oh, and what's your name?"

"Athena," the country girl replied. "And I met him in a storm. He gave me this, as a gift, to thank me for letting him in from the rain."

Wicklow was still sceptical. "And he told you to come to this exact café, to wait for someone off the boat who knew him?"

"He told me," Layla replied, with a note of nostalgia in her voice, "that one day, somewhere here in this city, I would meet a girl who needed my help. I would know her by the sign of the witch-rabbit. He said that if I helped her, she would go on to save the world."

Athena sat back, partly amazed, and partly disbelieving. "Really? To save the world?"

Wicklow brushed it off. "Yeah, I don't believe that either," he said.

"Well... maybe those weren't his exact words," Layla admitted. "It was a few years ago. Actually, I was twelve years old at the time. It was the day after my birthday. We had such a lovely party. But that's all as thin as the air, now. If you really are the one he told me to find – by the gods, you've come at exactly the right time."

"What do you mean?" asked Athena.

Layla leaned in closer to Athena and Wicklow, trying not to be overheard. "Things are bad, here," she said. "I mean, this is a nice café, and everything seems fine. But that's because all the merchants on this street can afford the protection."

She nodded in the direction of the street, just as a team of four men walked by. They wore black uniforms with golden shoulder sashes, carried muskets, pistols, and several kinds of blades.

"Those men are not the city watch?" Athena asked.

"No... they're mercenaries," Layla explained. "They work for one of the merchant princes. The city guard here doesn't do anything."

"But... this is one of the richest cities in the world," said Athena, uncomprehending.

"It is, but none of that money is in *your* hands, is it?" Layla said. "Go down any of the canals in any direction and you'll see houses falling apart, fires breaking out, and people dying on the street from dysentery and consumption. There are gangs of young men walking around, demanding money from everyone they meet, and starting sword fights when people don't pay. They say they're collecting taxes. And for all I know, they *are*. I'm telling you, in most of this city, as soon as the sun goes down, it becomes a completely different city!"

Wicklow sighed. "So, the city hasn't changed in hundreds of years."

"But there's a Movement," Layla said, whispering now. "We've got weapons, we've got money, and we've got people inside the council chambers, keeping us informed. We're almost ready to make a statement no one will ignore. And if you are everything Dubhdarra told me you'd be, we *need* you. Both of you!"

Wicklow looked to Athena, to gage how she reacted to this reality.

Athena said, "We already have a mission. We're looking to join the next ship leaving for Dawnland."

"Oh!" Layla said, taken aback. "Oh no! You mustn't go to the Scatterlands. Haven't you heard the stories? Wolves the size of houses, stalking the land. Rivers of acid and poison. Whole cities full of ghosts! Why in the world would you want to go there?"

"You might as well tell her; she won't believe you anyway," said Wicklow, grinning.

Athena glanced to Wicklow, and bit her bottom lip. "But is that true?" she asked. "Are the Scatterlands really like that?"

Layla reached out to Athena's hand. "Let me find better work for you, here in Port Vivaldi. My family has connections. And I can introduce you to Movement – you're not the only refugees from the army in our ranks."

"How did you know?" Athena asked.

"Gloves," said Layla. "But listen – anything you want, I've got it or I can find it. As long as it's here in the city."

Athena took a breath, to commit to her quest again. "We're going to Dawnland, to find the Gates of the Morning."

Layla covered her mouth with her hand, careful to preserve some kind of etiquette that Athena didn't understand. "You're going to – Well-a-well... that's beautiful. Let me show you something."

She rose, flagged down a waiter to pay the bill, then beckoned her two new friends to follow her. She led them down the wide cobbled streets of Port Vivaldi's central island, with its baroque-facade workshops and market halls, its decadent temples, and merchant-prince villas. Passing over a bridge to the next island in the city's archipelago, the streets narrowed, the cobbles lost their mosaic patterns, and the buildings lost their whimsey. Taverns replaced coffee houses; carpentry workshops and fishmongers replaced jewellers and perfumeries. More of the people they passed were drunk, and more of them made rude remarks to the three characters walking together.

"Didn't you say this part of the city wasn't safe at night?" said Athena.

"That's why I came with my bodyguard," Layla replied, as she took her new friends in her arms.

She brought them to a long quayside, where some of the larger ships were berthed. Though it was late at night, the area swarmed with longshoremen hauling barrels and crates up the ramps and into the ship's cargo holds. A train of horse carts arrived, each of them towing a wagon that carried a large cage. Inside each cage, Athena could see human faces and human hands. She could hear their voices, demanding release, refusing cooperation, crying for help.

"That's how you join the crew of a ship to Dawnland," said Layla.

Athena could only stare, gape-jawed, wide-eyed.

"Fuckin' hell – even I didn't know this," Wicklow said.

A crane on top of a high platform lowered its chains and cables to the ground. It was like the clanking and rattling claw of a strange mechanical creature. Workers attached them to the cages, then the crane lifted the prisoners on to the ships and lowered them on to a hatch on the deck of the ship, to be swallowed into the cargo hold.

"The city guard picks them up anywhere," Layla said, stepping back into a shadow to avoid the boat crew's attention. "Workers who can't pay the rent. Petty thieves and pickpockets, trying to feed themselves. Fringers who don't have their passbook on them. Anyone, really."

The last howls and cries from the last prisoners soon faded into echoes, then into silence, leaving behind the lapping of the water on the stone banks of the quay.

"Still want to go?" Layla asked.

Wicklow, however, considered the prisoners. "Does your Movement have a plan to *stop* this?" he asked.

Layla gave them both a secret knowing smile. "Aye, we do," she said.

Wicklow gave Athena a long look of consideration, as though asking permission to make a decision. Then he turned to Layla and said, "Perhaps we *can* accept your offer of a place to stay the night."

Athena consented with a nod.

Layla grinned. "Then let's go."

She led her two new friends away from the quay. They were almost at the end of the street where they could turn a corner and move out of sight, when Athena heard Sylvano shouting her name. He careened past them, almost tripping over his own feet to avoid knocking Wicklow to the ground. But he kept running directly toward the two guards at the quayside.

Two nearby guardsmen saw him running and raised their muskets. "Stop there," the first guard shouted. "By order of the governor, this quayside is off limits!"

"Shit!" Sylvano shouted. He wheeled around, looking for another direction to run. "Athena, you gotta help me, they're after me!"

"Who?" Athena said.

Three mercenaries from the tavern dashed into the square next, brandishing their swords. They spotted Sylvano at Athena's side. "Hiding behind girls and fringers now?" said Etienne.

Athena felt her face flush red with indignation at the sound of his words. Wicklow, too, scowled at them. They both drew swords.

"That one's a deserter," Etienne informed the guards. "If you turn him over to me, I'll cut you in on the bounty!"

Athena swapped her sword into her shield-hand, so that she could pull off her glove and reveal that she, too, was a deserter. "And if you try to *collect* that bounty on him, I'll cut *you*!" she threatened. She threw her glove at Etienne's feet.

Etienne smirked, enjoying the surprise, but his voice did not skip a beat. He addressed the two guardsmen. "That's a bigger slice of the bounty for you, if you help us," he offered.

"It's a deal," said one of the guardsmen. He blew his whistle, thus summoning three more guardsmen from the quayside.

Athena and Wicklow took their position on either side of Sylvano, protecting him. Sylvano, feeling more confident, drew his own.

Layla whispered to her three new friends, "Close your eyes."

"What?" said Sylvano. To Athena, he asked, "Who's your new friend?"

"Close them!" Layla hissed.

Athena, Wicklow, and Sylvano closed their eyes.

Layla reached into a slit in the hip of her dress, retrieved a grenade, and dropped it between the guardsmen and the mercenaries. It exploded with a bright flash, blinding everyone who still held their eyes open. A thick acrid-smelling grey smoke issued from it next, filling the street.

"Now run!"

Being unfamiliar with the lay of Port Vivaldi's streets, the three friends followed Layla's lead. Layla ran for the quayside, where the prison-wagons loaded their human cargoes on to the ships. She picked a small loose cobblestone up from the street and clubbed the first mercenary to recover from the grenade-shock. He fell to the cobbles again, out of the fight. Next, she stole his musket and used it to shoot the lock off the prison cage. The prisoners jumped out, glad of the rescue; Layla used them as a screen to hide the direction she ran to escape.

Athena, Sylvano, and Wicklow followed, pausing only to break open more prison wagons, as Layla had shown them. However, by that time, the guardsmen and the mercenaries were back on their feet. Some of them fired shots. The prisoners ducked low to avoid the musket balls. But the guards paid them no attention. They pushed anyone to the ground who stood between them and the four outlaws on the run.

By the time the hunters crossed the quayside, the four outlaws had fled the scene on stolen horses. They gathered at the foot of a bridge to the next island – a bridge barely wide enough for two horses at a time to cross.

"I see your new friend is resourceful," said Sylvano. Trotting his horse to Layla's side, he doffed his hat to her. "Sylvano Rizio, gentleman outlaw, at your service."

"Layla Darvi. Of the Poet's Lake Darvi," she replied. She offered him the back of her hand to kiss. Intrigued, as no one had ever done that for him before, he kissed it.

"We need to keep moving," Wicklow reminded everyone.

"Right," said Layla. "The Darvi family palazzo is two islands upriver. You'll know it by the sign of the witch-rabbit above the door. I had it carved there when I was seventeen, after the second time I met Dubhdarra. So that if I didn't find you first, you might find me. My uncle never believed the story. I think he agreed to the carving just to humour me. And a funny thing happened a few days after we finished it."

She stopped when they all heard the distinctive clopping of horse-hooves on cobbles, at a gallop.

"Move!" Wicklow shouted.

The four outlaws moved, just as four mercenaries riding stolen horses of their own galloped into view. They crossed the bridge, and somehow, with Athena in the lead.

"Which way, Layla!" Athena called out.

"Right. No, left!" Layla replied.

Athena veered left. The street narrowed; various parked wagons and small groups of people made it narrower still. A drunk didn't see Athena until it was too late for him to get out of the way and her horse struck him on the shoulder, knocking him through a window.

"*Now* go right!" Layla said.

Athena turned right at the next corner, still galloping at full tilt. The street widened, but the crowds of people thickened. Most were groups of young men on bar-crawls, still carrying their wine-goblets. Seeing the horses bearing down on them, they jumped out of the way, but shouted obscenities: "Watch it, you ass!" "Hey, slow down!"

Shots rang out. A street lamp took a hit, and its shattered glass rained down on Athena's head. She ducked and closed her eyes to avoid it. Taking a quick glance back, she saw the four mercenaries brandishing pistols and muskets.

Athena saw an opportunity. She climbed up on her horse, so that she was crouching on her saddle. At the right moment, she jumped up and caught the railings of a low-lying balcony. She used the momentum to swing herself up and land on the balcony on her feet. Then she drew her pistol and shot at the last mercenary chasing her.

He took the hit in the shoulder – enough to wound, but not to unhorse him. By the time he had taken aim to return fire, he had come almost under the balcony. Athena climbed over the railing and jumped on him.

The horse reared on his hind legs and slowed to a stop, while Athena and the mercenary wrestled each other for control. Athena won by banging his head on a passing stone wall, then unbuckling the saddle while he recovered. He slid off, his feet still tangled in the stirrups, and unsure of what had happened.

Athena turned around, grabbed the reins, and clenched the horse with her legs to hang on. She was now behind three mercenaries chasing her friends. The one in front of her had seen what she did. He twisted around to take aim with a throwing knife.

"Watch out!" she shouted at him, pointing at something ahead.

"Fuck off – you think I'm falling for that?" the mercenary laughed at her. Then the back of his head struck a hanging sign for a blacksmith's shop.

Athena took advantage of his momentary disorientation to ride up beside him and push him off his horse.

"Yes, I think you're totally falling for that," she said to him.

Her friends had been busy as well. Sylvano, who had a mercenary on his tail, caused his horse to skid to a near-halt and turn to the side, creating a wall for the next mercenary to slam into. He leapt off his horse and tackled the mercenary in mid-air, dropping them both to the ground. On their feet again, they drew swords. Sylvano lurched forward first and aimed toward his opponent's chest, not intending to hit, but rather to make the mercenary retreat a few steps. Enough so that the next mercenary, still galloping at full speed, would hit him, and take him out of the race. Sylvano grinned and took his horse.

Wicklow also had a mercenary on his tail. He decided to try and outrun his pursuer, trusting his knowledge of the city streets and their corners and curves, and betting that his horse had been trained well enough. He leapt over parked wagons and crates, twisted around the clusters of drinkers and drunks emerging from the taverns, while dodging the clotheslines and balconies that hung low – these narrow streets were made for pedestrians and not for horse traffic of any kind. But there was one kind of avenue in Port Vivaldi which Wicklow knew no one could use on horseback... the canals. Leaning forward to whisper a reassuring word in an ancient language into his horse's ear, he guided him toward the nearest bridge, and then veered to the side at the last possible second, to jump on to the canal-side path, and from there to jump on to the water. It bore them up. The horse's ankles splashing in the water as though they forded a shallow stream. When the mercenary who chased him saw this, he took only a moment to register this magical sight, this unexpected wonder. It may have been only a moment, but it was long enough for Athena to circle around and knock him off his horse with the broadside of her sword.

With their pursuers thrown off the trail, the four outlaws gathered in a small residential plaza. They dismounted and slapped their horses' hindquarters to make them run back to their stables. Then they took defensive positions at either side of the entrance, and behind a water-well, ready to ambush anyone who remained on their trail.

But no one came. They relaxed, and then they laughed.

"I think we got away," Athena cheered.

"So, where's this villa of yours?" Sylvano asked Layla.

"Probably not safe to go there, tonight," Layla said. "But I know another place. One more bridge to cross."

§ 18.

Carefully ensuring no one was waiting for them outside the plaza, the four crossed the island, and came to a gondola workshop. The light through the shuttered windows was dim, and the door was closed. It was an unusual sight compared to what Athena had seen of the city so far. The plaster had cracked and fallen away across much of the facade, revealing the rough-cast bricks and timbers beneath.

Athena noticed the winged rabbit carved in raised relief in a stone mantle above a door.

"This is a *safe house*, isn't it?" she realized aloud. "For your Movement?"

"It's not the family palazzo," Layla admitted, "but it's home."

Layla made two quick knocks on the door, paused, knocked once, paused again, then knocked twice again. A code, Athena surmised.

Several clunks, bangs, and shifts emanated from behind the door as various mechanisms were unlocked, and then it opened.

The man who stood in its frame was a full head taller than Athena. The lamplight came from behind him, making it hard to see his features.

Despite that, she saw he had dark, green-tinged skin, muscular arms, and sharp features. Sapling-twigs grew from his temples and his crown; leaves and berries mixed with his hair. The effect quickened Athena's heart, as though in the presence of a forest spirit and, as though at any minute, she might need to run.

"Layla," he said. "You can't bring strangers here." His voice was dark and low and resonant, like a cave. Some of his teeth were pointed.

Wicklow pushed his way forward upon hearing his voice. "Bailey – you're alive!" he cried, and he hugged him.

"Wicklow!" said the doorman, no less delighted to see him.

Sylvano and Athena traded puzzled looks. "So, they know each other," said Sylvano.

Wicklow turned back to his companions. "Bailey's one of my people, from my caravan. I thought they took everybody when they raided us!"

"I was away in the forest taking a shit," Bailey explained, laughing. "It's how they missed me."

They followed the green man down a short corridor of musty brick walls, lit with candles in small niches. Athena hesitated.

"You asked me to trust you with Layla," said Wicklow. "Now it's your turn. Trust me with Bailey."

"He's a – I mean, he looks like..." Athena didn't know how to say it politely.

"He's a fey-born," Wicklow informed her. "His father had a night of ignorant bliss in the woods with a dryad. Nine months later, baby Bailey was left in a basket at his door."

"In the army, they told us fey-born are demons of the abyss," Athena said.

Bailey heard that. "I think you'll find you can't always tell who the monsters are just by looking at them," he said.

He made another secret knock on a heavy wooden door at the end of the corridor. It opened, and they entered a wide room with a high ceiling. It was a gondola workshop by day, Athena guessed by the boats stacked on workhorses on one side, and the sawdust that built up like snowdrifts in the corners. Around thirty or more people sat around the worktables; she couldn't be sure how many, as her eyes adjusted to the dim glow of oil lamps and candles. Among them, there were people of more different shapes and sizes than she had known possible. Men with the heads of bears, panthers, and sparrows; women with the heads of foxes and rabbits. Some with ram's horns growing from their temples and curling over their ears. Others had oak leaves, birch twigs, or rowan berries in their hair – all fey-born, like Bailey. A white flag, with a green horizontal band running across the middle, hung from the rafters.

Several got up and welcomed Layla when she entered. "Friends," she addressed them, "Here's Athena, Wicklow, and Sylvano. They are refugees from the army. Athena... show them the gift Dubhdarra gave you."

Uncomfortable with the attention, Athena revealed the figurine of the winged rabbit.

"Hey, you found your hero!" Bailey said to Layla. To Athena he said, "We've heard her story about you so often, we were taking bets on who would be the first to tell her to shut up!"

"Were you really?" Layla said.

"We were taking up a *collection*," Bailey laughed. "Looks like Layla wins the pot, after all!"

Everyone near to Athena and Sylvano rose to shake their hands, clap their backs, and welcome them. Someone put a clay goblet in each of their hands. The barman was perhaps only three feet tall, and he walked on a special platform so he could remain at eye-level with everyone else. He took one look at the new arrivals, then nodded toward the coins stuck on the back of their hands.

"We've got someone who can get those cattle-brands off you," he said.

Athena agreed with a nod.

From a table in the far corner, a woman watched Athena and her friends arrive with silent but intense interest. Seeing the coin grafted on Athena's hand, she rose and approached. She swayed and lumbered as she moved, as though favouring an injured leg. She wore a horse rider's boots and breeches, and a long navy-blue coat. A white bandana kept her dark hair out of her face. A sword hung at her side, and her belt hung with a variety of pouches, sacks, and bottles. Her hair and nails were neatly trimmed, but her expression was dark and calculating. People paused their conversation as she passed near, lest they miss anything she might say or do.

She sat at a stool next to Athena, and with a gesture invited her to show her hand. She scowled as she examined the coin grafted to it. She sniffed it and scowled again.

"A shot of the oldest single-malt whiskey you have, if you please," she said to the barman.

"You need that to get the coin off?", Athena asked.

"No," she said. "You need to drink it. Because getting the coin off is going to fucking hurt."

Athena accepted the drink without hesitation.

The woman took a small wooden bowl from the counter and mixed some powders from her various pouches into it. "What's your name?" she asked.

"Athena Kildare," she said. "And you are?"

"She's Dane Blackwood. You've never heard of her?" said Layla, joining them. "Oh, but of course you must have. She was on the city council, once. In place of her husband, after he was lost at sea. The poor man. But our Dane – when she sat on the council, she was the only one who ever spoke out against the landlords and the merchant-princes. It's why she's not on the council anymore, as you can well imagine."

"That must have taken some courage," said Athena.

"Looks like you haven't had this very long," said Dane, examining the coin again.

"How did you know?" Athena said, amazed.

"I meet a lot of deserters these days," Dane said. "And when their brand is this new, it usually means they're not deserters at all. *They're spies*."

Athena tried to withdraw her hand, but Dane's grip was too strong.

"I'm not!" Athena said. "What the hell – let go of me!"

Layla intervened with a gentle touch, to loosen Dane's fingers. "She's no spy, Dane. I can vouch for her."

Dane ignored Layla. "How long have you known her?" he asked Athena. "Where did you first meet? How long have you been in the city? Who sent you?"

"That's enough," said Layla, her voice raised. "She's just a kid. The army picks up kids all the time. You know this."

Dane released Athena's hand and studied her face and posture for a while.

"They took my whole family when I was twelve," Athena told him. "They took Sylvano, too. He's from the same village as me. Wicklow was a prisoner… we took him with us when we escaped."

"Where was your camp?" Dane asked.

Wicklow said, "A week's travel, to the north-east. Close to the border with Stagsland."

"What banner did you fly? Who was the camp commander?"

Athena glowered at him. "You still think I'm a spy."

"Look around you," said Dane. "Everyone here had to escape from something. A bastard landlord, a prison-farm, a violent drunk in the family. What about you? I can tell it's not the army. What are you *really* running from?"

The seriousness and darkness in Dane's tone of voice told Athena she might kill her if she didn't like the answer.

"Not so much running *from* something, as trying to *find* something," Athena told her. "A ship to take us to the Gates of the Morning."

Dane perked an eyebrow. "Really," she drawled.

Athena said, "I want the gods to explain to me *why* there are bastard landlords and prison farms. And why they don't do anything about it. Wouldn't you like to know that too?"

Dane made a condescending chuckle, then checked herself as he saw

Athena was quite serious. Then she spat into her bowl, to make a paste out of the powders she had mixed there.

"The gods won't fix the world. They need it to stay broken," she said. "Because the worse things get, the more we pray. And the more we pray, the stronger they get. And the stronger they get, the more they fuck with the world to make us pray. A vicious circle. Best to ignore them and do whatever you need to do to survive. You ken me?"

Athena relaxed her shoulders. Much as she believed Dane was wrong about the gods, still it seemed she had decided she was not a spy.

Dane applied the paste to the edge of the coin. Athena let out a shriek and squeezed her hand on a bar towel to resist the pain, but she did not flinch. Dane smiled, approving of her self-control.

"Don't touch it until it doesn't hurt anymore," Dane advised. "Then the scab should come off by itself. You'll have a scar for a few weeks, and the bounty hunters will look for that, too. So, keep your gloves on."

"Thank you."

Before letting her go, Dane said, "There comes a time in everyone's life when they have to choose. Whether to observe the world, or whether to *live* in it. Whether to *complain* about injustice, or to *fight* it. We here in this workshop... we've chosen to fight. What will you choose?"

"I just quit one army; I don't want to join another," said Athena.

Dane acknowledged the point with a nod and an open hand. "Fair enough," she said. "But you should know we're going to make something happen here. Very soon. Something that will get the attention of those powdered heads who think they own this city. If it succeeds, it could change everything. Maybe for all of Summerland." She leaned forward and made her tone low and final: "If you truly believe you're here to save the world, this might be how you do it."

Athena studied the rolling of her whiskey in its cup as she swished it around, thinking about these words.

Dane turned to Sylvano, tapped the back of his hand, and said, "Your turn."

§ 19.

Layla caressed Sylvano's hand, almost but not quite touching the chemical burn where the coin once grafted to his hand.

"Two years, you've had this?" she said to him.

"Plus a few months," Sylvano confirmed, with a grin. "And now, I appear to be a gentleman outlaw. What do you say to that?"

"Gentleman outlaw, eh?" Layla said. "Well-a-well, you've got the outlaw part down pat. We can work on the gentleman." She extended the back of her hand to him. "So... first lesson. What should you do when a lady shows you the back of her hand?"

Sylvano grinned. "Something like this, maybe?" he said. He took her hand and kissed it.

Layla smiled with him. "Very good," she said.

Athena sat down between them, not noticing that they had been holding hands for a while. "There's no other way to go to Dawnland, is there?" she asked.

"You could buy your own ship if you were rich enough," Layla told her. "But Dawnland... it's like being away with the Whisperlights forever! Of all the places in the world where you could go, why there?"

Athena sighed. "I wanted an answer to... something," she said, her voice quiet and uncertain.

"I've been thinking about that question of yours, Athena," said Sylvano. "Maybe you don't need to go all the way to Dawnland, to get an answer. Maybe we could do some good *here*, in Port Vivaldi."

Wicklow, joining them, shook his head. "What do you want to do?" he asked. "Reform the council? Kill all the lawyers? Whatever you have in mind, it's been tried before. And it didn't work."

"Why not?" asked Sylvano.

Wicklow said, "Because every time there's a revolution, the new leaders turn out to be just as bad as the old ones. The first thing they do after they win, is purge the ranks of everyone they say isn't loyal enough.

Then after that, they stir up another war. And, if anyone doubts it or questions it, they get shipped off to Dawnland."

Layla, who had been shaking her head at Wicklow, said, "Dane Blackwood is different. She won't be like that."

Wicklow scoffed at her. "I like her. But how can you be sure about her?" he asked.

"Because I know what she's planning," Layla said.

"What? Can you tell us?" asked everyone around the table.

"There's a town in the western cantons, called Lavender Hill," Layla explained. "And there's an army, laying siege to it with a score of cannons, thousands of soldiers, and even a few sky-ships. They told us the siege had gone on for more than a year. Yet somehow, the besieging army was *losing*, and the town was winning!"

"Incredible!Amazing! How?" said their listeners, who now included a people from nearby tables.

Layla said, "The defenders were not fighting to change one king for another. No more kings. No more jealous gods. 'Summerland belongs to all' was their motto. They declared the town a commonwealth. Where everybody *votes* for their leaders. Everybody – fringers included! They made a charter of rights and freedoms. There'd be no secret trials, no arrests without charge, no forced labour, and no forced childbearing. The best part... no one above the law! The high-and-mighty have to follow the same rules as the rest of us." She pointed to the flag hanging behind the bar. "See that? That's our banner. The white of the old regime, with the green of Summerland running across it, pushing the old world away."

About half the room was listening to Layla now. Their voices grew excited and hopeful. "We should have that here," they said to each other.

"That *is* the plan," said Dane, rising from her stool at the bar, her sonorous voice cutting through the din.

"And we're hearing that it's not just Lavender Hill," Dane added. "The biggest cities in the western cantons... Highbridge, Port Gaeleach, and The Watch – they've joined the Commonwealth, too. Up in Kellsland, the city of Rath Macalla joined. The Movement is not only growing, it's winning!"

Cheers of agreement and excitement filled the room.

"Our city is the biggest, the richest, and the most powerful in the whole of the Thousand Valleys... maybe in all of Summerland," Dane said, as she took a central stage in the room. "If a small town full of druids howling at the moon can fight the united forces of a dozen tyrant kings, *and win*, think what *we* could do here!"

The excitement grew. People slapped their hands on the tables and smiled, imagining what they could do. Dane grinned to see it.

"So... this is the plan," Dane said. "Our city is built on dozens of islands. This one, the one we're standing on, has only two bridges. One goes to the next island, the other to the north shore of the mainland – a strategic position. That's why, tomorrow, at noon..." she raised her voice again, to gather her ideas all together, " we will *barricade* those bridges..." she paused, as the crew gave her louder cheers, "we will declare this island part of the Commonwealth..." more cheers, louder still, "and we will hold it until reinforcements arrive. After that, we take the city!"

The crew in the tavern gave her their loudest ovation.

"Summerland calls!" Bailey announced, rising to his feet and raising his cup.

"And we shall rise!" The crew recited back. Some jumped on the benches, some clapped and hugged each other, pledging themselves to the fight. Dane started up a rebel song. Others who knew it joined him. Feet stamped the floor, and wine-cups stamped the tables, keeping rhythm.

Layla took Athena by the hands. "Fight with us, Athena," she said. "Tomorrow could be the day you save the world."

Swept up in the spirit of the moment, Athena smiled. "I will," she said, though she also looked down to the floor.

Layla hugged her and handed her a cup of wine. Wicklow lifted her on his shoulders, so she could play-fight with swords against Layla, who had climbed on to Sylvano's shoulders.

Dane leaned back on the bar and smiled like a proud victorious queen.

§ 20.

Athena awoke the following morning in a room above the workshop, to the sound of the market-calls from fishmongers, butchers, and fruit sellers in the street outside. Sunlight streamed in through a window, warming her face and hurting her eyes. Several others lay in the other beds or on the floor, still asleep.

Sylvano, she noticed, shared a bed with Layla. All their clothes lay on the floor.

Still dressed in her shift and her woollen stockings, Athena donned a dress and a bodice and tied a linen belt around her waist. Looking around, she could not find her boots. She crept downstairs to search for them, and for something to eat.

The space last night, that had been a tavern, was now reverted to a boat workshop in the morning. Two gondolas lay upside-down on sawhorses where the tables had been. Workers applied a foul-smelling caulking to the grooves between their planks, to waterproof them. Others worked at a carpentry station, cutting new planks for hulls, benches, and carving new paddles. Athena recognized some of the workers from the previous night. Bailey greeted her as he saw her, though he did not pause in his work. Beer tankards and wine cups, some still half-full from the night before, lay on the bar but several baskets of fresh fruit and bread lay among them. No one objected when she took an apple for herself.

Dane Blackwood sat on a stool behind the bar, examining an accounting book and several purses of copper and silver coins. She waved for Athena to come closer.

"Athena. Good morning," she said. She pushed a bowl of plums across the bar to her. "Hungry?"

Athena took one of the plums. "Where did all this fruit come from? It's all out of season," she said.

"We've a stockpile in the icehouse, downstairs," Dane explained. "One of our supporters is a druid who put a spell on it, so things stay fresh down there for longer. Coffee? I don't imagine you got coffee in your army camp."

"In fact, we did," Athena said, smiling. She poured a cup for herself from Dane's pot and drank. "Can't wake up without it."

"Well then, camp life wasn't so bad, yeah?" Dane said.

Athena sipped her coffee and chose not to answer.

Dane leaned forward. "How would you like to do the most important job in the forthcoming... what shall we call it? Festivity?"

Athena put her coffee down. "What job is that?"

"Firing the first shot," said Dane, as she sipped her own coffee.

"The first shot?"

"Strictly speaking, you'll be launching a *signal*," Dane explained. She leaned closer, so that the workers on the boats would not hear her and spoke low. "You'll stand in the watch tower over the bridge that leads to the next island. Then wait until you hear the noon-day gun from the roof of the governor's palazzo. After that, you'll watch for guardsmen crossing the bridge, coming on to our island. They'll be in a group of two or three; they'll never be alone. And the moment they set foot on our cobblestones, you will launch a rocket."

"A rocket!" Athena exclaimed, excited.

"It's all prepared for you," Dane promised. "The fuse line, the launcher, the flint and steel. You'll fire it straight up into the sky, where it will explode. The whole city will hear it."

"Why do you need me to wait until the guards cross –"

Dane hushed her with a finger to her lips, then invited her to come closer. "Because we're going to take those guards as *hostages*," she said.

Athena wasn't sure how she felt about that part of the plan. "I see," she said.

Dane placed a wheel-lock pistol on the bar. "I assume you know how to use this?"

"I do," Athena said.

"When our festival is on, the authorities might send a sky-ship, to drop the imperial guardsmen behind our barricades," Dane said. "If you get a good shot on anyone on deck, take it."

Athena took the weapon. "Sylvano's much better than me with these things. My dance partner was always the blade."

"You can take your pick from our collection," said Dane. She nodded toward one of the boats in the workshop, which was covered in a linen blanket. Athena uncovered it and found it full of muskets and rapiers.

"Take another apple, too," Dane offered.

Athena took another apple. Thinking about Dane's plan as she ate, something occurred to her. "Last night you thought for a while that I might be a spy," she said.

"A real spy wouldn't have a cover story as outlandish as yours," Dane said, smiling.

"But if there *was* a spy in the room last night," Athena said, "then why tell everyone the fight begins at noon? Why give away your plan?"

Dane scowled and regarded her in silence for a moment. Athena wondered if she was about to accuse her of being a spy again.

"Because everyone in the room last night is *loyal* to me," Dane said. "They will not peep a word of what I said to anyone. Not even to their own families. They know what will *happen* to them if they do."

Athena felt some of her hair stiffen and rise.

"Everything has been planned and prepared for weeks," Dane added. "But I must thank you for joining us when you did. Your flying rabbit has the people believing the gods are on their side."

Athena clutched the figurine under her shift.

Their side, Athena noted her words. Not *our* side. Something felt wrong about that.

"Layla will take you to your station," said Dane, and she dismissed Athena with a wave.

§ 21.

The vista from the narrow platform on top of the watchtower gave Athena a secret view of everyone crossing the bridge. Market carts, horses, buskers, and beggars crossed this way and that – the whole of Port Vivaldi's life passed by beneath her tower. In another direction, her post provided a good lookout of the island's interior. In its wider streets and tenement courtyards, children played hopscotch and tag while the adults drew water from the cisterns, or hung the laundry on the lines to dry. To see them, without being seen by them, and without their knowledge was a strange feeling! As if uncovering a secret – perceiving their truth. How precious and fragile it was, and the sense of responsibility she felt it conferred.

At the same time, Athena held in her hands the power to disrupt their lives forever – the flint and steel to light the fuse. It would launch the signal to begin the rebellion. *Am I about to burn down this city*? she wondered. *Like the colonel burned my village, all those years ago*? *Am I about to kill hundreds of people*?

The noon-day gun boomed across the city. With it, clusters of men emerged from the shops and tenements and gathered by the foot of the bridge or by the plaza's exits. They seemed to take great interest in the street-side art hawkers and cordwainers. Dane's vanguard, Athena realized; they had taken their posts, and awaited her signal.

The first guards to cross the bridge were part of a team that surrounded a well-appointed carriage. They were three to a side and armed with muskets. The curtains on the carriage were drawn, but Athena surmised by the polished brass ornaments and the driver's velvet coat that the passengers were people of privilege.

She picked up the flint and steel, ready to ignite the fuse line. A simple flick of the wrist, taking no effort at all, and the world would change. A shudder passed through her belly. She could delay the signal by a few heartbeats, but no longer than that. She hoped it was enough to seal into her memory a picture of the world before it ended.

In the street below, someone with a long coat and white bandana bowed her head at the carriage as it passed her. But her eyes gazed past the carriage and up the tower to Athena. Athena realized her view of the world was not so secret, after all. The plan must have included a few people whose job was to make sure other people did their jobs. The watchmen were themselves under watch. Perhaps the gods were watching, too.

She lit the fuse line. The little flame followed the cord up to the rocket's nozzle, creating a thin white trail of smoke that smelled of sulphur and finality.

The rocket launched into the sky. It exploded with a deafening shockwave that rattled every door and window on the island and sent most of the people below into fits of fearful screaming. In the same instant, a dozen of Dane's men rushed to the carriage. For each of the six guardsmen surrounding it, there was a man who came up from behind him and buried his head in a burlap sack, and another man who punched him in the stomach and stole his musket. The move was swift, confident, and perfect – Athena thought likely they had rehearsed it. The driver whipped the horses into a gallop, hoping to escape but someone leaned out of a second-storey window along his escape route and shot him. All part of the plan.

People poured out of every door in the plaza below, carrying benches, tables, and chairs. They piled them along the foot of the bridge; a barricade, just as Dane had promised. Once the furniture from the taverns and shops had run out, they grabbed the market carts out from under their owners, to add to the pile. They threw in crates, barrels, and bundles of firewood; they even took shutters off windows, and doors out of their frames. With that, a gondola from the workshop joined the affair. In less than a minute after Athena's signal, the bridge was closed. When the men were satisfied with their barricade, they raised the white and green Commonwealth flag on it and raised their muskets and pistols to defend it.

The rest of the island emptied. Those not involved in arming the barricade had dashed away into hiding, and a silent tension took hold of the world. Athena stood up to take it all in. This transformation of things, and this nervous anticipation, was all created with her rocket. She produced a spyglass to watch for sky-ships. This was the second duty of her post on the tower. The other towers in the city had the same trade galleons and passengers' schooners arriving and departing – traffic as usual, it seemed so far. Some of the ships moored to towers were designed like birds, leaves, or geometric shapes, with sails below the keels as well as above the decks. There were creatures of the sky that could never berth in the water.

Movement from below caught her attention. The carriage had been taken to a tenement courtyard, along with the six guardsmen who once protected it. Their heads were still under the sacks, and their hands were tied behind their backs. The woman with the dark hair and white bandana forced the occupants out at the point of her pistol: two women and one man, dressed in silk finery in bright colours. They too, were bound and bagged, and pushed against a wall beside their guards. One by one, they were tied to a horse hitch.

And then, one by one, the woman with the dark hair and white bandana slit the women's throats.

Athena gasped and turned away. She caught her breath. Then she looked again, as though to make sure she had seen what she had seen. She soon realized she might be the only witness to the murders.

The well-dressed man from the carriage, Dane did not kill, but bundled him back into the carriage, still in his bindings.

Athena decided she no longer had any reason to follow Dane's orders. Taking up her weapons, she dashed down the tower and into the plaza. The fighters ran supplies to the barricade: musket cartridges, barrels of gunpowder, and crates of home-made grenades.

"Where's Dane?" she shouted.

"She took the hostages to the catacombs," said Bailey, running by with an armload of muskets.

"She *killed* the hostages – I saw her do it!" Athena said.

"No, I don't believe it," Bailey retorted. "Didn't you hear her last night? She's completely single-minded. Committed to the cause. She's –"

The flight of the carriage, with Dane for its driver, interrupted Bailey's praise. The horses careened at full speed out of the courtyard and down a boulevard toward the island's other bridge.

"She's abandoning you!" Athena told him.

Bailey dropped some of the muskets. "Why would she do that?" he wondered aloud, still disbelieving.

Before Athena could answer, someone from the barricade shouted, "Here it comes!"

A deafening bang sounded from across the bridge. A cannonball smashed through a chair on the top of the barricade, sizzled through the air an arm's reach above Athena's head. It ploughed into the front face of a guild hall, across the plaza, smashing a crater in the wall. Razor-sharp stone shrapnel from the crater lacerated the nearby rebels. They shrieked with surprise and pain. Blood-scars ripped across their arms, faces, and legs. Children and elderly folk fled the neighbouring buildings, in search of safer shelters.

Athena ducked into a door-frame for shelter from the shrapnel. When she felt it safe to stand up again, Bailey was gone; frightened by the battle, she assumed. The muskets he had carried lay in a pile where he dropped them. Sylvano and Layla dashed into the plaza. Sylvano saluted them with his hat. "Sorry we're late. But in our defence, the coffee was excellent. We had to savour it," he said, grinning.

A second cannonball crashed into the barricade, throwing fragments of tables and benches into a debris field, slamming into the wall on the opposite side of the plaza, and showering everything in stone shrapnel again. Amidst the wreckage, someone staggered into Athena, unable to see where he was going, as the shrapnel had blinded him. He pawed the air and slapped his bloody hands on Athena's shoulder.

Athena shrieked. The others backed away from him and looked around for somewhere to hide from the next cannonball.

Athena picked up Bailey's pile of dropped muskets and put one into each of her companions' arms. "You're just in time to take over where Dane left off," she told them.

"What do you mean?" Layla asked.

"She's gone," Athena told them.

They loaded their weapons and took positions at the barricades, closer to its ends so that the keystones of the bridge might protect them from cannonballs. Glancing over the top, Athena assessed the enemy's strength.

"They've only two cannons," she said. "Small ones – four-pounders. But enough to clear a path through the barricade."

They watched the gun crews load a new cartridge into the barrels and compact them with a ramrod.

Sylvano chose his moment. Closing one eye and steadying his aim, he fired. His shot struck one of the gun crewmen in the back of the head, sending blood and bone in a spray. He dropped the cannonball, and it rolled to a harmless stop at the foot of the barricade.

Sylvano dropped the musket and grabbed the next one, primed for him already. Steadying his aim, he fired on the second gun crew. The ball struck the soldier who was holding the cannon wick. He dropped it on the stack of gunpowder cartridges. The crew, seeing this, rushed away to avoid the coming explosion. When it came, soldiers and cannonballs and cobblestones erupted together, ending the crew.

Sylvano tipped his hat to them, and grinned.

By that time, the first cannon crew got its next shot ready. Sylvano saw this, and found he had no more ready-loaded muskets. The cannon fired, and the ball slammed into the barricade near the middle, adding to the damage from the previous shots, and making a hole large enough for the enemy to break through. The ball carried on through the square, bouncing on the cobblestones, spraying flakes of stone around it, then smashing down the guild hall's front door.

Soldiers ran forward, hoping to take position before the defenders were ready to fire. The barricade's defenders regrouped, with muskets primed and ready.

"All together in a volley," Sylvano commanded. "Wait for them to cross in front of their cannons. Hold... hold... Fire!"

A dozen muskets fired at once. Athena, her friends, and the other defenders who were ready in time, had taken their shot. Most of the soldiers in the first line of attack facing them fell.

Athena smiled at Sylvano, proud to see him learning how to lead.

But more soldiers behind the fallen were ready to charge forth and take their places. Athena judged the distance they had to run. They would reach the barricade before she could reload.

"No time for a second volley – we have to fall back," she told him.

Sylvano agreed. "Fall back!" he called.

The defenders scrambled away, looking for any corner, door, or shelter where they could reload in safety and fire on the barricade. Layla, however, took a grenade from a crate.

"What are you doing? Fall back!" Sylvano shouted at her.

"I only need one!" she told him. She lit its fuse and dropped it back into the crate.

Sylvano grinned; he understood her idea. He fired a pistol-shot at the on-rushing soldiers, taking one down, and frightening the others. Then he and Layla ran around the back of the sentry tower.

As a team of soldiers climbed through the hole in the barricade, Layla's grenade exploded. It triggered every other grenade in the box to explode with it. The blast threw everything near it into the air: tables, barrels, gondolas, and soldiers.

The defenders cheered, but the bridge was now wide open. The remaining cannon crew also had a clear line of sight to fire on anyone in the plaza.

Some of the defenders fired on the cannon crew, but they were too far away now. Most of their shots ricocheted off the cobblestones and missed their marks.

Then a shadow crossed the plaza, accompanied by a low rumbling. A sudden breeze blew a cloud of stone dust and wood chips into the air. Athena looked up. A three-masted galleon hovered over the plaza, approaching the battlefield from behind.

"In here!" Athena shouted to her friends, thinking that the guild hall might provide cover from both the cannons on the bridge and the bombs dropping from the sky-ship.

Her friends joined her whereas most of the other defenders scattered. "It's over, we're routed!" Athena heard one of them say.

She sprinted into the guild hall and up the stairs to its top floor, in search of a vantage where she could watch the plaza below and the sky-ship above.

Huddling beneath a window whose glass had been broken in the fighting, Layla said to Sylvano, "When you were in the army, did they teach you how to bring down a sky-ship?"

"Only way to do it is with another sky-ship," Sylvano said.

"That's a lot of help," Wicklow snickered.

The ship loomed low over the rooftops. Its crew hung several ropes over the sides. A team of soldiers slid down the ropes, landing on the rooftops. Once on their feet, they cocked the hammers of their muskets and looked around the streets and the rubble below for a target. Athena and her band of outlaws crept around the balconies and ladders, looking for a way up to meet the new threat on a level battlefield.

Sylvano recognized their black leather jerkins and gold shoulder-sashes. "Volscraggers," he named them.

Wicklow agreed. "They'll shoot every fringer they can find."

Athena glanced at Wicklow. She squeezed her friend's hand. Looking to Sylvano and Layla next, she said, "Then we stop them."

Without waiting to see if her friends would follow, Athena scrambled up a wall and on to the roof of its neighbouring tenement. Drawing her pistol first, she shot the nearest mercenary.

The next mercenary fired back, but Athena jumped to the side at just the right moment. The bullet glanced off her shoulder pauldrons. Before he could reload and fire again, Athena was close enough to draw swords and disarm him.

"Not letting *her* have all the fun," said Sylvano. He, too, climbed the wall and reached the roof. A third mercenary, seeing him charge, opened fire. Sylvano ducked and the bullet knocked his hat off.

"Hey!" Sylvano shouted at him. "Sorry, but it's the city guard's turn to try and kill me today. You can take your turn tomorrow."

Sylvano had no shortage of other mercenaries to duel. Nor did the other rebels – Athena, Layla, and Wicklow each had an opponent chasing them. The footing on the roof was never sure with angled landings, broken or breaking tiles, and walls crumbling from cannonball damage to imperil every step. Wicklow selected a long pole for his weapon; possibly an axle from a broken market cart. He wielded it like a quarterstaff and was parrying, feinting, and riposting with it. It also proved useful for bracing himself when a roof-tile crumbled, or gave way beneath his boots. Layla carried a pair of daggers, one in each hand and, with them her opponent found her defence impenetrable. Daggers could catch blades in their quillons as easily as rapiers. However, her opponent kept out of the reach of their tips with his longer sword and his buckler.

Athena, facing off two swordsmen at once, found she had to retreat to keep safe. Where she might have had an advantage fighting one of them, the other could twist in and find the hole in her defence to strike home. Her defence lay in retreating to a rooftop too narrow for both of them to reach her at the same time. Finding one, she faced off with the first swordsman to follow her there. Then, by twisting, thrusting, and parrying, Athena finally struck her mark. The assailant slid down the roof, his armour and boots clattering on the roof-tiles, dislodging some of them on the way. He fell to his end on the cobblestones, more than three stories below. Athena had no time to confirm that he was dead as the second swordsman came at her from behind. She twisted to avoid his first thrust, but the blade caught her on her side, slicing through her armour, and drawing blood. She cried out and staggered back. The smiling mercenary seized the initiative to strike again, feinting toward her injured side and then thrusting high, toward her face. A slit appeared on her cheek. Behind her, the roof came to its edge and the nearest building was too far to jump. The mercenary seemed to know this and he need only push forward to let her fall and win the fight.

Athena ventured a quick glance to her friends. Each was engaged with a foe of their own, and some in positions no less precarious. Further, she could see the sky-ship coming about, with sharpshooters on the deck taking aim. She dropped to the roof and slid down, landing on a balcony one storey below. The move caused more blood to flow from her wound. Knowing her enemy would follow her, she broke down the balcony door and dashed inside, to find a place to hide.

As she ran from room to room, it occurred to her that she had one more move that her attackers didn't know about. Finding a corner where she could avoid being seen, she grasped her winged rabbit figurine and whispered into its ears: "I need your help again. And so do my friends. I'm wounded, and I might not make it without you."

She staggered down the stairs to the ground floor. It was a single open room – kitchen, pantry, and dining room were all in the same space. The window-shutters and doors were gone; likely they had been taken to reinforce the now-destroyed barricade. She could run across the plaza, but she would surely be seen by the sharpshooters on the sky-ship and the city guard on the bridge. The heavy boots of the Volscragger who had wounded her tromped about on the floor above. She would soon be found. She backed herself into a corner and, with shaking hands, attempted to reload her pistol.

Movement caught the corner of her eye, outside the house. A rabbit with white fur, red eyes, and grey ears, emerged into view. It regarded her for a moment, then it hopped across the plaza, spread its wings, and took to the air.

Athena grasped the figurine again and said, "Thank you."

She wasn't yet out of danger. With her pistol reloaded, she prepared for the mercenary to descend the stairs. His ankles appeared, taking each step slowly. Then his thighs, as he crouched down with his own pistol at the ready. When Athena saw his head, she fired.

The shot struck the mercenary in the shoulder. Blood swelled under the linen of his sleeve and he returned fire. Athena rolled out of the way in time and, with nowhere else to hide, she dashed out of the house. Athena was wincing with the pain of her wounds, hoping to find somewhere to take cover before the sky-ship crew spotted her. She found it in the remains of the barricade – one of the soldiers from the cannon crew saw her take shelter there. He strutted toward her with a malicious grin that made Athena want to shoot him. Weakened from blood loss, she could not muster the strength to stand and fight, and the soldier could see that. He took his time loading his musket, smiling, and lining up the shot. He fired.

Dubhdarra's firm hand caught the musket-ball in mid-flight. The astonished soldier made a guttural noise, unable to put his surprise into words. When he recovered and remembered his training, he fixed a bayonet on his musket and charged.

Dubhdarra reached out and caused the weapon to fly out of the soldier's hands and into his own. He broke it across his knee, as though it were a twig, and threw its pieces to the side.

The soldier, now terrified, ran away.

Dubhdarra checked to see if Athena was safe. Then, he jumped up three stories into the air to land on the rooftop where Athena's friends were still locked in duels with the Volscragg Gentlemen. He found them grouped together. It was seven mercenaries versus three rebels, with the mercenaries poised to force their adversaries off the edge of the roof, to fall to the street below.

At first, the mercenaries paused to see what side of the battle Dubhdarra would take.

"Who the hell are you?" said Etienne.

Layla recognized him: "Dubhdarra! You're back!"

Dubhdarra winked at her.

Etienne pressed an attack, hoping to take advantage of the distraction of Dubhdarra's arrival, and force him off the roof too. The ranger anticipated this. He made a gesture, causing a flock of ravens to rise from behind another building, and swarm about the mercenaries. They swarmed, pecked, scratched, and bit the men without mercy, drawing blood, and tripping their feet. Swordplay became impossible.

"Witchcraft!" Etienne accused, through gritted teeth. "Sorcery!"

"Retreat! Retreat!" The other mercenaries shouted. They withdrew, searching for a safe way off the roof, while squinting their eyes and batting their arms against the flock.

"Dubhdarra, the sky-ship!" Layla warned.

Dubhdarra saw it. He equipped his bow, nocked an arrow to its string, and loosed. The arrow struck the ship in its hull, making the kind of hole that a cannonball would make. An explosion rocked the ship, sending a fireball up through the top deck, and igniting its sails ablaze. The panicked crew steered the ship away, in search of a safe place to land.

Sylvano stepped back. He made a fist with his thumb between his two middle fingers and drew a circle in the air; a ward of protection he had seen his mother use.

"That doesn't actually work," Dubhdarra said to him, grinning.

Sylvano lowered his hand. "Who are you?" he asked.

"An old friend of your mother's, as it happens," Dubhdarra said. "Now, shall we join Athena?"

They jumped down as far as was safe for them, landing near the ruined guild hall walls, from where they could climb to the plaza again. They found Athena sitting up, and pressing her hands down on her wound, struggling to contain the bleeding.

"Let me see that," said Dubhdarra. He examined it for a moment, then pressed his fingers into the flesh above and below the cut. Athena winced. The bleeding stopped. He traced his fingers along the length of the cut, sealing it, and leaving a slight scar, as though the wound had been inflicted and healed many years ago.

Athena, wide-eyed and awestruck, sat up straighter. "You came for us," she said, when she found her voice again.

"You chose a wonderful moment to call for me," Dubhdarra said, grinning. "Now, let's get off the street, before the rest of the army comes looking for you."

§ 22.

The remaining rebels gathered in the gondola workshop, now empty but for themselves. They sat in a circle on the floor, leaning on the ceiling-posts. Cups, plates, and bowls lay scattered about where people had fled in haste, taking furniture to the barricade. Apples, plums, and bread rolls mingled with sawdust and the Commonwealth flag lay crumpled on the floor in a corner. The late afternoon light streamed in from the canal and the river-mouth beyond, bringing the smell of seaweed and foam as Layla stared off to the distance, shrugging away Sylvano's attempt to caress her shoulder and comfort her. Wicklow made finger drawings in the sawdust on the floor whereas Athena unbuckled her leather armour, tossing it aside.

"Had anyone told me the story, I wouldn't have believed it," said Wicklow. "But I saw it for myself. That carriage was loaded with money. Hundreds of gold coins... millions, in banknotes. And some rich guy was being held as a prisoner – I think it was the governor."

"Could someone else have done it?", Layla asked. "Someone who wasn't in on the plan, and just got swept up in the moment?"

"I saw her do it," Athena mumbled.

Layla waved her hands in the air. "I just thought," she said, stumbling on her words, "I really believed I would be free of everything today... and I could start over."

Sylvano said, "Does the Movement actually exist? That place – what's it called? Lavender Hill?"

Dubhdarra, who had been feeding the seabirds and the fish in the canal, turned round and said, "Yes, that part is true. There *is* a Movement to break the spiral of tyrants. Seven cities have joined it, so far."

"Were they going to send us reinforcements?" Layla asked. "Did they even *know* about us?"

Dubhdarra shook his head. "No," he replied, in his most compassionate voice.

Athena threw her pistol aside in frustration. "Maybe the gods *enjoy* watching us struggle," she mourned. "Maybe they think our failures are *funny*."

"Your struggling breaks their hearts," Dubhdarra said, his voice soft and sincere.

"How would *you* know?" Sylvano accused him. "And, while I'm at it, who are you? How do we know you won't betray us the same way Blackwood did? Whose side are you on?"

"I am on the side of Summerland," Dubhdarra said.

"Not a helpful answer," Sylvano grunted.

Dubhdarra acknowledged it with a tilt of his head, and a grin. "The oldest stories say the gods intended Summerland to be beautiful. A place of safety and peace for everyone; a sheltered harbour in the endless cosmic ocean. So, when I say, I am on the *side* of Summerland, I tell you I am on the side of everyone who needs Summerland to be that harbour. The side of everyone helping to make it so."

"If that's true, said Athena, "then, how did it come to this? Where did it all go wrong?"

"That, I believe," said Dubhdarra, with a grin, "is what you wanted to go to Dawnland to find out."

All eyes looked to Athena.

"It's true," she told everyone. "I wanted to find the Gates of the Morning.

Sylvano and Wicklow have already agreed to come with me. Layla, maybe you might want to come too?"

"Why don't we go to Lavender Hill?" Wicklow suggested. "Continue the fight. The real one."

"We *have* to go to Dawnland," Athena insisted. "If we go anywhere else, we'll be followed. Or we'll make new enemies. I don't want to live the rest of my life on the run. Do you?"

Her friends only stared at her, unmoving... but she could tell that they agreed.

"You can't just *go* to Dawnland," said Layla. "And it's not only because you need a ship."

"I don't follow..." said Athena.

"You've heard people say that, in the Scatterlands, you can't land on the same island twice," Layla said. "That's because they're not like normal islands. You come to one of them, and it's a nice sandy beach. You think you're safe. You come back to the same island next year, and it's a jungle full of giant spiders. You come back the year after that, and it's a swamp. And the year after *that*, it's gone; it sailed away. The Scatterlands follow their own natures. Nobody's ever figured them out... except for the Navigators."

Everyone turned to Wicklow. Dubhdarra perked an eyebrow at him.

"I still need a map," said Wicklow. "And I believe..." he looked at Layla, "you might have one."

"Me? No," said Layla.

"In your family's cabinet of curios?" Wicklow suggested.

Layla realized that Wicklow might be right. "My uncle once told me – maybe I shouldn't have told Bailey; he can't keep secrets – my uncle told me his grandfather had been to Dawnland. He'd been there and returned, many times. He could do it because he had a Navigator on the payroll. And a map."

Dubhdarra rose and gave Athena a fatherly rub on her shoulder. "I believe you have things in hand, Athena. Everyone here knows the choice they have to make. We will meet again."

Athena touched his hand, to say goodbye.

As he passed Wicklow, Dubhdarra leaned into his ear and said: "You need to tell them."

Wicklow looked back at him, puzzled, but did not reply.

The ranger left the workshop. The sound of his footsteps faded into the background of the city. Athena gazed long in the direction of his parting, then felt the beginnings of a new plan take shape in her mind. "Well then. Anybody up for some mischief, tonight?"

The excitement she expected from her friends did not appear.

"Obviously, we're going to have to *steal* it!" Athena told them.

Her friends looked to each other, waiting for someone else to speak first.

§ 23.

Athena traded her hat for a long rough-spun cloth, which she used as a head-wrap and a veil to cover her hair and her face. Feeling safe from the city watch and from the Volscragg mercenaries, she wandered the city for a while, getting to know the layout of its streets, islands, and canals, taking a mental note of useful landmarks: gondola docks, bridges, and horse stables. All possible escape routes.

From listening to people talking in the street, she learned that her battle at the barricade was not the only fight that took place in the city that day. Less than half an hour after she had launched the rocket that started the rebellion, a large professional army entered the city from the south, attacked the defenders from their rear, and captured the governor's palace. The damage from the battle lay around her with buildings smashed by heavy cannonballs and bodies buzzing with flies on the cobblestones. Teams of workers were cleaning it up. Walking on, she found a crowd had gathered in the square in front of the governor's palace to celebrate the downfall of the old ruling family, and to meet their new masters. The flagpole on the roof flew the same banner Athena had seen at the camp. It was blue, with the raging wolf head, and a white crown.

A dozen men stood on the palace belvedere, enjoying their adoration.

Most, Athena assumed, were the middle or high-ranking officials in the new administration and all of them were uniformed military men.

One of them was Etienne d'Orsonnes. This struck Athena as strange. Didn't he fight against the fringers, and help put their rebellion down?

Another familiar face was Colonel Patroclus Crave, the camp commander. A face she had hoped she would never see again. But as she thought about it, his presence made sense to her. He must have commanded the force that took the palace.

It was the sight of a third person, dressed in a Volscragg sash and strutting behind the other peacocks on the stage, that chilled her blood: Dane Blackwood. Smirking and swaggering, she treated herself as every inch the equal of the others on the belvedere. And they, in turn, smiled to see her, and clapped her shoulders to thank her for doing her part. As Athena's blood pressure rose, the full significance of that day's events clarified in her mind. The battle of Fringer Island, as the townsfolk had come to call it, was not a rebellion – it was a diversion. It had been planned that way from the beginning. Dane was the infiltrator whose masquerade was so perfect that the Movement made her its leader.

"People of Port Vivaldi!" Colonel Crave announced. "Your exiled leader has returned! And to thank you for your most generous welcome, I give you the usurper, the tyrant-king of the East Cantons... in his true nature! Not a god, not a king, not even a man, but a creature of the Abyss, who fed upon your hard work as a vampire feeds on your blood!"

The ground-level doors of the governor's palace opened. Four guards emerged, holding between them an elderly man clad in nothing more than a loincloth. He was gagged at the mouth. His posture attempted at strength and dignity, but his face was defeated and afraid. Athena recognized him as the man from the guarded carriage whom Dane did not kill. More pieces of the day's puzzle fell into place.

One of the soldiers behind him pushed his head into a helmet, and clamped a metal mask over it, giving him the head of a dog. The soldier locked the helmet-mask over his head, so no one could remove it. The man certainly tried.

"Do with him as you will," Colonel Crave invited the assembly. The soldiers pushed the man into the crowd. And the crowd rushed at him, clubbing him with walking-sticks and rocks, screaming and laughing in exultation.

Athena suppressed an urge to vomit. She fled the square, and found a quiet corner where she could remove her veil for a moment and breathe.

When she recovered, she found herself standing across the road from the Darvi family palazzo, looking up at its four stories of baroque windows, parapets, and belvederes.

She took a seat at a nearby empty café with a good view of the palazzo's front doors. When evening descended, she noticed several couples and small groups arriving there. Dressed in some of the richest and most ridiculous costumes she had ever seen, the guests also wore white porcelain masks with elaborate wigs and hats. The Darvi family was hosting a masquerade.

This, Athena thought, would make infiltrating the palazzo easier – if she had a costume. She recalled passing a costume shop earlier that afternoon, so she returned to it, and found it closed.

She didn't have enough money for any of its wares anyway but she had a stiletto. It was just the right shape and size to pry open the shop door, like a crowbar. Glancing about the street, nobody seemed to care what she was doing; plenty of shops had been damaged or looted during the day's fighting.

Once inside, she selected a dress and a shoulder-cape that could conceal a weapon or two, as well as a hat big enough to contain her curls. She chose a mask, expressing the face of a young woman in mourning. It had a painted blood-red tear falling from its right eye.

"Seems appropriate," she said, as she fitted it on.

She approached the palazzo from an alley where the servants came and went. There she found a small courtyard full of empty market-carts – perfect for hiding her rapier and her musket-rifle. Her stiletto and her pistol she hid inside her skirts.

Coming around to the front of the building, Athena slid herself into line with a cluster of other guests, moving as though part of the same group. The concierge at Palazzo Darvi's front entrance did not even look at her.

Too easy, she thought to herself.

She followed the flow of party guests to a ballroom. The room was adorned with elegant chandeliers, marble walls and columns, oil-painted portraits of merchant-princes and their families, and golden sculptures atop white-marble pedestals. A chamber orchestra at the far end of the hall played an up-tempo waltz and waiters in black-and-white uniforms and white wigs served wine to the guests. The guests sipped them through the mouths of their masks using straws.

Watching how the women around her moved and greeted each other, she observed how to hold her own hands, how to carry a fan, and how to curtsey – all social graces no one had shown her during time in the army camp. The move that troubled her most was how to accept a kiss on the back of her hand. She worried that someone would feel the scar on the place where the coin had been removed.

"Athena?" someone whispered. Athena pretended not to hear.

"*Athena*!" the voice whispered again.

She looked, while trying not to appear to look. A slim young man wearing a yellow jacket, waistcoat, and breeches, approached. He wore a curly grey wig, a tricorn hat, and a fox mask.

"I know it's you," said the fox. "You're the only lady in the room wearing army boots instead of heels."

Athena realized she recognized the voice. "Layla?" she asked.

"And you don't *move* like a lady," added Layla. "You can't curtsey properly – even the boys in drag know how to do that."

"I grew up in the army," Athena explained. "Is it really that obvious?"

Layla said. "Let's just get you out of here before anyone else notices."

She took Athena's arm like a gentleman and led her to a corridor elsewhere in the palazzo.

"I didn't think you were going to come with me on this," Athena asked.

"We *had* to come," Layla said. "We knew you'd be a disaster if you came here by yourself."

Layla led her to a room that housed a taxidermy collection. There were scores of small animals stuffed with sawdust, posed, and set in their display cases with a dozen or more heads of larger animals mounted on the walls. Many of them belonged to species Athena had never seen nor heard of before. A cat-like creature with porcupine quills? A lizard that walked upright on its hind legs, like humans do? And there was what looked like a wolverine with sharp bony plates emerging from its spine.

Her first sight of the Scatterlands.

The centre of the room featured a taxidermied gazelle, whose tawny gold coat shimmered and glowed with ethereal light, illuminating the room. Its antlers, likewise, seemed made of solid bronze. A label on the plinth read: *Dawnlandic Gazelle*.

"Grandfather brought some of these gazelles home from Dawnland, still alive, to breed them," Layla said of it. "See how they make their own light? It's how they attract mates, during the rut. There are people who ransom whole castles to buy just one of these pelts, to weave the fibres into their clothes. It's what made my family rich."

Athena ran her fingers through the fur. "Soft as silk, too," she observed. "You gave up all this to join the Movement? To fight for fringers' rights?" Athena asked her. "Why?"

Layla took her mask off. "If I had stayed here, my uncle would have controlled every minute of my life. I'd have to live in his house, agree with all his opinions, and go to all his parties. I'd have to smile and be pretty for his fat-headed friends and their spiteful, selfish wives. Or laugh at their stupid jokes, and pretend it's no bother when they slap me in the ass. Uncle would insist that I marry one of their sons, too. All the luxury and comfort I could want, in trade for never having a minute to myself."

Athena took off her mask and regarded the gazelle as Layla spoke. A magnificent animal, a wonder to behold, but frozen in time as if in a trance, imprisoned in its own flesh to satisfy the vanity of others. Its dignified expression covered a hidden despair, the same which Athena now recognized in Layla.

"But come," said Layla, some of her former cheerfulness returning. "What you're looking for is probably down here."

Layla put her hand on a small wooden carving of a dragon, on a shelf behind the door. It was posed as if listening for a nearby danger. Athena checked that the corridor outside was empty, then Layla twisted the dragon on its base. A knocking noise issued from a nearby bookcase. Layla pushed the bookcase open, and grinned.

A dark corridor, and a downward-sloping stairway, appeared before them. Layla lit the oil lamp provided on a niche in the wall.

"I'll wait for you up here, and warn you if anyone comes," Layla said, then closed the secret door.

The stair led down to a crossroads of underground chambers. One looked like an alchemy workshop – an oven lay on one side, and a workbench cluttered with bottles, phials, and powder jars stood across from it. A second chamber seemed to be a storeroom with barrels, crates, and burlap sacks piled up on heavy timber shelves. Athena opened one of the sacks and found it full of golden gazelle pelts. The family strategic stockpile, she surmised.

The third chamber was another cabinet of curios like the room above. But here, most of the treasures were kept in locked glass display cabinets. These, Athena presumed, were the things the patriarch of the family revealed to only the most trusted friends. Among them, flat on a table in the centre of the room, and almost as large as the table itself, lay a map. It showed all of Summerland: a vast continent with the Heartwater between them to the east, the Thousand Valleys to the west, two parallel mountain ranges to the north and south, and the outlying provinces above and below the mountains. Measuring with her hands, she guessed that the whole of Summerland was some nine hundred leagues, from east to west.

A cabinet built into the table contained more maps, filed and labelled in a script she had never seen before. Other labels were translated however, and among them, a name stood out.

Dawnland.

She stole the folder under that label, and rolled it around her leg to stuff it into her boots. Retracing her steps upstairs, and careful to make as little noise as possible, she pulled the bookcase open and closed it behind her.

Only then did she notice Layla was backed into a corner of the room, while two people stood over her, masks off, holding her at gunpoint. It was Etienne d'Orsonnes and Dane Blackwood. Athena put her mask back on before they noticed her.

Etienne cocked his pistol and pointed it to Layla's face. "Mask off, now!" he demanded.

Athena grabbed an antlered skull from one of the display shelves and clubbed him on the head with it from behind.

Dane turned to see who the attacker was. The move was enough to allow Layla and Athena to dash out of the room. Dane drew her pistol and fired. The ball pierced a hole in the door frame.

There was no place to hide in the corridor outside; their only option was to keep running. Another shot was fired, and someone screamed. Athena risked a quick look over her shoulder. Etienne and Dane were chasing her now, guns drawn, arms pushing people off their feet and out of their way. Athena fled in the direction that she hoped would lead to the palazzo's back door, and the weapons she stashed in the rear courtyard.

The first door she threw open was a study. Bookshelves and portraits lined the walls, and a large desk dominated the centre of the room, where several men pored over an accounting ledger and several purses of gold coins. Athena turned to get direction from Layla but found that they had gotten separated in the crowd. Dane was gone too, presumably chasing Layla; Etienne, however, was close to Athena's trail.

Throwing door after door open, Athena soon found a kitchen, and a path to an exit. She threw pots, cauldrons, and serving trays off counters and ovens to create obstacles for her pursuer. Furious kitchen workers hurled every profanity they knew upon her. It did not stop Etienne, but it slowed him enough so that Athena could fly out the back door and slam it shut behind her, before he made it halfway through the kitchen.

Once in the courtyard, Athena toppled a stack of crates in front of the door and retrieved her rapier and musket. With seconds to prepare, she dropped a market cart on its side to serve as a barricade, and prepared a line of fire with her musket, trained on the kitchen door.

Etienne and Dane burst out of the villa together, each brandishing a pistol in one hand, and a rapier in the other.

Athena fired. Her assailants saw her weapon just in time to dodge out of the way, and so her shot struck a wall. Athena ducked under the cart to avoid the volley of return-fire that was sure to follow. One shot hit the wood, splintering it but she heard no second shot – someone was waiting for her to lift her head up again. So, she somersaulted away, leaving her spent musket behind. The second shot rang out as she dashed down the lane, smashing into a window behind her, shattering the glass into daggers.

She found herself in a blind alley. There were no escapes save for locked doors or windows that were far too-small. There was not enough time to climb up the walls and escape over the roof. Etienne and Dane sprinted into the courtyard.

"Mask off!" Etienne threatened again, with his rapier poised to strike at Athena's throat.

Athena threw her mask off, revealing herself.

"Kildare!" Dane recognized her.

Athena raised her own rapier to her.

Dane smirked at it. "Allow me to introduce you to my associate, Etienne d'Orsonnes, a gentleman of means and leisure," she said.

"Gun for hire, you mean," Athena taunted, but then they turned their fencing blades at Athena again.

"Now come with us," said Etienne. "You can come peacefully, or not. But you *will* come."

Athena looked around the courtyard. Like most residential courtyards in Port Vivaldi, it had a water well in the centre, a few balconies with ladders leading to them, and little else. She side-stepped around its edge, looking for a better position. Etienne and Dane followed, still out of striking range with their rapiers, but a single pace forward would close that distance. Their eyes fixed on her, daring her to strike first.

Athena reached up with her shield-hand and pulled a lever that hung down from a balcony. A ladder swung down, striking Dane in the shoulder. Etienne retaliated with a leap ahead and a thrust with his sword.

Athena parried as best she could. With the odds against her, she knew she had little chance to go on the attack. She moved to keep the well at the centre of the courtyard between her and her opponents. Dane moved slower than Etienne, she noticed; an old injury that she had seen her favour before. When Etienne leapt over the well to attack with momentum, Athena lost the protection she had. In exchange, albeit for a fraction of a second, she gained a chance to swipe at his ankles. The move worked and Etienne landed on his hips, giving Athena a chance to dance out of reach.

Dane, however, stood her ground near the courtyard's exit. Athena would have to duel her to escape, while watching her back for when Etienne got on his feet again. So, she advanced swiftly, flashing her steel almost at random, aiming to disorient her quarry rather than to strike. This startled Dane; she parried in the wrong direction several times, and soon found herself on the back foot as Athena moved in past the tip of her rapier, close enough to stab her with a dagger. Dane pushed her off with her elbow but Athena used the momentum to grab Dane's rapier by the blade close to the cross guard, to attempt to disarm her. She only succeeded in pulling Dane off balance and neither let go. Dane drew a dagger in her shield-hand to seize advantage again. Upon seeing the blade, Athena pushed her away, using her rapier to trip Dane as she stepped back. She fell on her bottom, astonished.

But now Etienne was back in the fight and drew a second pistol from a hidden holster, and fired. The shot struck Athena's dagger, flinging it out of her hands. Etienne reloaded the weapon faster than Athena thought was possible.

Athena decided that the time had come to flee the scene. She ran, jumping over Dane on the way, avoiding a wild slash with her dagger.

On the city streets again, Athena threw off her shoulder-cape and hat, and stole a hooded cloak from a drunk stumbling out of a tavern. It was enough to enable her to hide in the crowd.

Dane and Etienne, searching the crowd for Athena, grabbed the wrong woman by the shoulders.

"Watch yourselves!" the woman shrieked at them.

Seeing some nearby city guardsmen take an interest, Dane and Etienne walked away.

§ 24.

Athena found a quiet corner on one of the city's outlying islands, with a good view of the north shore, its muddy beach, and the farm fields beyond. With the two moons nearly full, and a street lamp nearby, she had just enough light to examine her stolen prize. She checked first to see that no one was observing her. Then she removed the map from her boot and unfolded the treasure within.

To her surprise, the parchment depicted a menagerie of animals, monsters, and gods, contained in a system of radial coordinates: a map, not of islands and coastlines, but of constellations and stars.

Have I stolen the wrong map? she wondered.

She gazed into the night, into the darkness beyond the city. Along the edges of the water, and over the wildflowers in the farm fields past the shore, a spread of fireflies meandered in the air. But no, she decided; they were not fireflies, but *Whisperlights*, all sun-gold, ocean-blue, cedar-green, cloud-white, and blood-red. A more magical name for a thing of wonder.

Contemplating them, the clopping of horses in the city behind her diminished, as did the distant laughter, singing from the taverns, and even the gentle washing of the waves on the shore. Soon, it was quiet enough to reveal a subtler sound. It was distant and fragile, like the crickets, frogs, and peepers of the evening, but softer, as though such creatures played the strings and woodwinds of an orchestra, or sang long and sonorous magic spells in a language she did not speak. And yet, Athena knew its meaning, or perhaps she felt it, for it was the sound of her own anguish, her indignation... her despair. The theft of seven years of her life became the alto notes of the ethereal choir. A taste of freedom among the high-minded rebels of the city, dashed away in a swift and easy defeat, became the baritones. And the soprano voices descanted the path forward in the map she held in her hands but could not read. Whatever strange eldritch things these Whisperlights might be, they *knew* her. They gathered her in, tears and all, for now she was weeping; they clustered around her, and blessed her.

An old gondola was tied up nearby. Its paint was peeling and ornaments had long since fallen away from decades of bumps and knocks with quay sides and moorings. She climbed in and paddled across the river, the fairy-colours of the Whisperlights reflecting on the water as much as they glowed in the air, surrounding her with love, below and above.

For a moment, she remembered Wicklow had warned her against

following the Whisperlights as she might return somewhere else in the world, far from the city, or far from anywhere she knew. She might return after what seemed like minutes or hours, to find she had been missing for days or weeks. However, she also recalled Dubhdarra's summation of the world – *the gods intended Summerland to be beautiful*. And here, in this night, and in the hour of her despair... it was.

Climbing on to the far shore, she found a place to sit. The Whisperlights surrounded her. They were still too small to see, even when one landed on her fingertip, and she held it close to her eyes.

She became aware of someone approaching, silent as a breeze, and sitting down on the grass nearby. The visitor was a shadowy shape at first, but soon in the glow of the lights, the form became clearer. Athena saw a woman of about the same age, with the same hair, height, and ensemble of bodice, skirt, and hat. The woman wore the same mask Athena had earlier, when she stole the map.

Startled, Athena drew back. The visitor held up a finger to her mouth to call for silence. Then she held out her hands, to ask for the map.

Athena clutched it close to her chest at first, but the ghost was patient and waited for Athena to decide she was not in danger. When she was ready, Athena handed the map to the apparition.

She examined it for a moment. Athena pursed her lips, unsure whether to welcome or to dread what the visitor might say about it.

"Why do the gods allow terrible things to happen to good people?", the visitor said. She spoke with Athena's own voice, but somehow older, and coming from above and below, and all around. Athena felt her heart jump again. Her hands closed into fists and covered her chest in protective reflex.

"That was your question, was it not?", the woman asked. "Have you thought about what might happen if the gods *answered* you?"

"They're the *gods*," Athena said. "Whatever answer they give, it'll be the truth. It'll *have* to be."

The ghost perked her head, examining Athena's heart, assessing whether Athena herself believed her own words.

"There are only three possible answers to a question like yours," she said.

"The gods are *unable* to help, or they're *unwilling* to help, or they *don't even know we need* help."

"It's impossible they don't know we need them," Athena said. "They're the gods!"

"That leaves the other two answers," the visitor reasoned.

"I can't believe the second one either," Athena said. "The gods *created* this world, didn't they? Creating is a kind of caring, isn't it? We care about the things we make. So, so surely the gods *care* about the world. They *have* to care about what happens here. It would be *insane* if they didn't!"

"Perhaps they *don't* care," the ghost suggested, "and that's why they don't intervene."

"I refuse to believe that," Athena declared.

"That leaves the last option: they're *unable* to help," said the visitor. "But if that's true, does it even make sense to call them *the gods* at all?"

Athena thought about this for a moment and realized that she didn't like the implications. "You're trying to confuse me," she said, with growing ire. "Who are you, anyway? What do you *want* from me?"

"You want me to decipher this map for you... show me how far you've thought it through!" The ghost told her. "Summerland has seen a great many young heroes who set out to save the world. And those who succeeded – and they were very few – it wasn't long before they became the very tyrants they overthrew."

"I'm not the same as any of them," Athena insisted. "I'm not even a warrior. I'm not trying to save the world. I only want my questions answered."

"Very well, then," the ghost said. "Steal a sky-ship. Fly into the sunrise. Demand your answers from the gods. It almost doesn't matter *what* answer they give you. Half the world won't believe you. And the other half will think you're making all the problems of the world into *their fault*. And they will hate you for it."

"Some will believe me," Athena countered, committed to winning the argument.

"Indeed... some will," the ghost agreed to Athena's surprise. "But soon those believers will come to want something from you, that you won't be able to give."

"And what's that?"

"More answers."

Athena hadn't thought of that. But she did not want the ghost to know it. She pursed her lips, and fingered the figurine of the winged rabbit, hanging in its safe place between her breasts.

"Do you even know what evil *is*? Or where it comes from?" the fairy-woman asked, her tone growing more aggressive. "How can you ask the gods to do something about it, if you don't know what it is?"

"Isn't it *obvious* what it is?" Athena shot back. "It's everything that's happened to me!"

"That's what *everyone* says. What makes your pain so special?"

"It's mine!"

The ghost paused. Athena's answer, though born of frustration, was at least the only answer she knew even if it was not the answer she was looking for.

"What will you say if the gods have questions for *you*?" said Athena's double, under the mask. "What if they asked you... Why did all those things happen to you? Is it *human nature* to be terrible to each other? Or is it *the world* that's somehow broken? Did the gods create us this way, or did something happen to us? How do you fight the tyrants without becoming one and what do you do if it turns out that's not possible? And... I ask again – what if the gods give you an answer that you don't want to hear?"

"I don't know," Athena mumbled.

"Say that again?"

"I don't know!" Athena howled back.

The ghost acknowledged it with moment of calm, and a solemn nod. "That is an *honest* answer," she said. She opened the map, and held it up to the sky, to match its coordinates with the stars themselves.

The sky was partly cloudy, and the moons washed some of the stars away with their glare, but Athena could make out two or three constellations well enough. Some of the stars on the map were below the horizon. Others in the sky did not appear on the map at all. The Whisperlights themselves filled in the spaces, made the shapes of the constellations' animals and heroes in the sky, and extended the map beyond the parchment's edges.

Like the unfolding of a flower inside her mind, the map became a story.

With that, Athena perceived the way to the Dawnland.

§ 25.

Layla hissed at the spike of pain in her battle wounds, as Sylvano wiped them clean with a whiskey-soaked cloth. Then he dabbed a layer of honey over her wounds and wrapped them in a bandage.

"The honey slows the inflammation and prevents gangrene," Sylvano explained.

"I've never met a gentleman outlaw who knew how to dress a wound," said Layla, as she pulled her stockings back on.

"I suppose I'm not much of a gentleman, am I?" Sylvano asked, grinning with embarrassment.

"I'm glad you're not," Layla said, shifting closer to him. "I don't want any more gentlemen in my life. I want friends, now – poets, thinkers, dreamers, and fighting partners. Real people... like you."

"Like me?" Sylvano asked, imagining himself as she saw him.

"The way you stood up to fight with us," Layla explained. "The way you took charge at the barricade, when Dane ran away. Dressing my wounds, like this. Touching me, like this."

They sat together on the floor of the gondola workshop, amid the remains of the rebellion. Sylvano dipped his finger in the honey pot and invited Layla to lick it off. To his surprise, she did.

"If I'm not a gentleman outlaw, I have to find something else to be," Sylvano admitted, smiling but sad. "But what? I didn't come to the city 'seeking my fortune', like other people do. In fact, I came here to kill someone."

Surprised by this admission, Layla almost laughed. "To kill someone?"

"The man who took me and Athena from our village when we were kids," said Sylvano.

"So, you came to the city for revenge," said Layla.

"Athena doesn't know," Sylvano said.

Layla examined him for a moment – assessing his posture, facial expression, and the way he held his hands as he told his story.

Then she smiled and said, "How can I help?"

§ 26.

Athena burst into the gondola workshop, breathless and exhausted. She immediately faced three gun-barrels, as Sylvano, Layla, and Wicklow took aim at what they thought was a city guardsman come to arrest them. Athena removed her veil and revealed herself.

"Athena!" they gasped together, delighted to see her. They helped her to a place behind the makeshift barricade of gondola hulls they had built in the workshop. "Where did you go? What happened? No one followed you, I hope?"

By way of her answer, Athena removed the stolen map from her boot and handed it to Wicklow.

"How did you… never mind, it's better that I don't know," Wicklow said, amazed.

Sylvano looked at the map over Wicklow's shoulder. "This is a *star map*," he complained. "We're as good as dead."

"I know how to read it," said Athena. "It shows the exact positions of the stars, on Midsummer midnight, as seen from a place thousands of leagues from here – as seen from the centre of Dawnland. We can calculate the distance and direction by comparing the stars on the map to the stars right above us."

With this explanation, Athena's friends perceived the map differently.

"Wicklow, is that true?" said Layla.

Wicklow meditated upon the map for a moment. "I'd like to borrow this for a few hours, to make the calculations," he asked Athena. "I have to factor for time, as well as for distance. By the way, how did you figure it out?"

Athena said, "I went into the Whisperlights."

Wicklow gasped. "You went into – I can't believe you did that," he said.

Athena smiled and shook her head. "See, Dubhdarra gave me all kinds of different advice every time I saw him. The most important was the advice I didn't even know was advice at all. *Don't be afraid*. It's the first thing he'd say, almost every time I met him. I realized tonight that, for most of my life, I've been afraid of *something*, and miserable because of it. But tonight, I went into the Whisperlights anyway. They spoke to me and, now I'm not afraid of anything... not even of going to Dawnland."

Sylvano, feeling a little chagrined by Athena's words, sat up straighter and said, "Well, I've *never* been afraid of anything. Nice to see you catching up!"

Athena winked at him and said, "That's why you're coming, right?"

Sylvano realized he had fallen into Athena's trap. He grinned to cover his embarrassment.

"But you still need a ship," Wicklow reminded everyone.

This time, Layla sat up. "That," she said, "I think I can help with."

§ 27.

Wicklow crossed the bridge from the island to the north shore but stopped near its middle. He leaned on the balustrade, holding the map in his hands, rolled like a baton. He tapped it against his chin, thinking about it, as he took in the view of the night sky.

"Good to see you, brother," said Bailey, approaching from the opposite side of the bridge.

"Find a buyer for this yet?" Wicklow asked him, holding up the map.

"Yeah, I got a buyer," Bailey confirmed. "He's agreed to meet us tomorrow. And he's offering enough for us to buy our own ship, if you wanted one. Thing is – are you still willing to sell?"

"You think I asked to meet you here to talk about the birds?" Wicklow said, his voice stern.

"It looked like you were having second thoughts," Bailey said.

"Not at all," Wicklow said without hesitation. "If I took those three kids to the Scatterlands, they'd figure out the truth on the first day out."

"Of course," Bailey said, understanding. "Out of curiosity, though, how *do* you become a Navigator?"

"You have to go into the Whisperlights," Wicklow said. "Like my father did."

"I hear that kid Athena had a night among the lights," Bailey said.

"That's what makes no sense to me," Wicklow said. "Why did she come back in an hour, and my father, not at all? How could she walk into the lights like it was easy, whereas I – an *astron*…"

The fey-born shrugged. "You'll have to ask her, not me," he said. "But for now, come on down to the pub. Your only choice tonight, really, is wine, ale, or cider. I know what I want – how about you?"

Wicklow followed his friend back to the city. "I'll decide when I get there," he said.

§ 28.

"My uncle has a private sky-ship," said Layla, as she escorted the outlaws across the city to the Darvi family palazzo. "We call it a yacht but it's really a schooner. He used to take me out on trips over the Heartwater, and sometimes up to the mountains. Once we went out all the way to Anatellios, on the edge of the Great Eastern Sea. Have any of you ever been? The wine there is so wonderful and plentiful. And so cheap! Oh, but do any of you know how to sail?"

When everyone said, 'no', Layla said, "That's okay, we have a crew on the payroll. All we have to do is give the orders, but you'll have to let me play captain; none of the crew will know who you are. I'll just tell them that you're investors in the family corporation. They won't know the difference anyway."

"Didn't you tell me the other day," said Athena, "that you wanted to *leave* your family? And now you're going to talk your uncle into giving you the family yacht?"

Layla sighed and made a helpless gesture. "He'll be glad to see me," she said. "I was always his favourite. He says things about me like, 'That Layla Darvi – she's the real head of the family!' Oh, and I must tell you about the time he took me on one of his hunting trips in the countryside. I was thirteen years old. That was when I learned how to fire a musket. I actually shot a pheasant on my first try! Can you believe that?"

Athena smirked at Layla, knowing that her cheerfulness was a mask.

The guard recognized Layla and opened the door to them. They made their way to the study. Athena kept her head down, hoping her hat and hair would hide most of her face.

"Best if you let me do this by myself," said Layla. "Especially you, Athena, in case Dane or Etienne told him you were here last night."

Athena agreed. Her friends waited in the corridor.

Layla knocked on the doorframe, and stepped half-way into view, adopting a demure and apologetic expression.

Inside the study, Layla's uncle looked up from his books and papers. "Layla!" he said. He dropped his quill on the desk. "Returning to us, wings clipped, and tail between your legs. Just like I said you would."

In the corridor outside, Athena whispered, "Her uncle – it's him!"

They exchanged a wide-eyed, desperate look. Sylvano's fingers reached for the hilt of his pistol.

"What are you doing!" Athena hissed at him.

"Getting our honour back," he replied.

"Sylvano – don't – please," Athena told him.

Wicklow agreed with Athena. "You'll never get out of here alive if you do," he said.

"I blew my first chance; I'm not blowing this one," Sylvano told them.

Athena moved to leave as quietly as she could. She tugged on Sylvano's arm, but he brushed her off.

Wicklow followed Athena out of the palazzo, giving Sylvano a disapproving glare on her way. When they were gone, Sylvano primed the wheel-lock of his pistol, and prepared himself.

In the study, Layla nodded but kept her eyes down. "Everything you warned me would happen if I left the city, happened. And here I am."

Colonel Crave rose from his desk. "Running off to the wilderness with the fringers, calling it freedom, and then finding yourself swept up in a romantic insurrection that you ought to have known would fail," he said. "I trust you learned your lesson?"

"I have, Uncle," Layla told him.

"We were *afraid* for you," said Crave, compassion entering his voice. "We sent our sailors across the city to look for you – we thought you might have been killed!"

"I almost was," Layla admitted. That much, she reminded herself, was true.

"Well. It is good that you made your way home at last," said Crave kindly. "Of course, you understand, you caused quite the scandal when you left. People thought we couldn't keep our house in order. We lost clients… we lost business."

"I know how to make it up to you," Layla said, raising her head and meeting his eyes.

"Oh?"

"One of the new friends I made out there, is an *astron* Navigator," Layla declared with pride.

"Really?" said Crave, nonplussed. "You must have travelled far indeed."

"I met his whole family," Layla said. "Their caravan camped with us for a while. They told me of a place in the Scatterlands that had the same kind of gazelles like the ones in your collection. I thought, what if they were talking about the same place – the *exact* same place?"

Crave perked an eyebrow. "And you think your new friend knows the way?"

"I know you can't spare any of the Navigators who already work for you," said Layla, smiling now as she delivered what she hoped would be the winning argument. "So, let me take the *Sun Dog* –"

"My personal yacht!" her uncle chortled.

"With me as the captain," Layla proposed. "And my own Navigator to find that place again."

"That would be a very expensive expedition," said Crave.

"But much *less* so than a fully outfitted three-year mission in a square-rigger with full crew," Layla said. "I'm asking for a smaller ship, with a smaller crew. We won't need a whole year. In fact... I think I can do it in four months."

"Only four months?" Crave asked, intrigued. "A wonder of nature is the idealism and ambition of youth."

Layla smiled. "If we don't find it by then, we turn around and we come back home. I swear to the Great Queen! But four months is plenty of time in the Scatterlands. Just think what *else* we might find on the way! The voyage will almost certainly turn a small profit even if we *don't* find more of your gazelles."

"The Scatterlands are unpredictable. You might come back empty-handed, or not at all," the colonel reminded her.

"Living with the fringers, I learned how to protect myself," Layla said. She played with her skirts enough to show that she had two daggers hidden there.

"So, I see," the colonel said.

Sylvano peered around the doorframe to assess his chances. He could see Layla from behind, but not her uncle. He saw the walnut panelled-walls, candle sconces, and oil-painted portraits. A battle-plan formed in his mind – he could march three paces from the door to the desk, take the shot while still possessing the advantage of surprise, and run out.

Layla sat in a chair beside the desk. "It gave me a lot of time to think about what I really want in life, and what really matters to me," she told her uncle, as Sylvano listened. "I made some hard choices but I also made some new friends. Including – maybe I shouldn't tell you this – I met a boy who… well-a-well, I think he's in love with me. And I think I'm in love with him, too."

Sylvano, hearing Layla speak of him this way, closed his eyes. His battle-plan grew tangled.

Colonel Crave made a patronizing grin. "Interesting. Does he come from a good family?" he asked his niece.

"He was in the army for a while," Layla said, hoping that answer would be good enough. "And he's willing to come with me to the Scatterlands. Who among those useless pretty-boys at the salons would do that? Some of them can't even tie their own shoes."

The colonel conceded with a quiet chuckle that Layla had a point. "Isn't that the truth," he said.

"And he's kind," Layla continued. "He listens to me. He stands up for me. He knows what he wants in life, and he's not afraid of anything. And I love him."

In the corridor outside the office, Sylvano lowered his weapon and rubbed his eyes to dry them of their tears.

§ 29.

"We got it!" Layla told her friends waiting in the courtyard outside the palazzo. Then she noticed their worried faces. "What?" she asked them.

"We have to leave as soon as possible. That's all," Athena said.

"The *Sun Dog* will be loaded and ready by tomorrow morning," Layla assured her. To Sylvano, she said, "There's still enough time to do *that thing* you wanted to do, before we leave."

"It doesn't matter now," Sylvano said, shaking his head and not meeting her eyes.

"I don't understand," Layla said. "You had such a strong sense of purpose yesterday, and a just cause. What happened?"

"I can't tell you," Sylvano said.

But Athena said, "I can."

"Don't," Sylvano advised her, his voice desperate.

"We have to," Athena admonished him. Choosing her next words with care, she said to Layla, "It's about your uncle. He knows us. We can't let him see us."

"How could he possibly?" said Layla. "He spends most of the year in the wilderness, where he's the commander of –" She stopped herself, as she realized how Athena and Sylvano could have known him. "Oh," she said.

Athena said, "He put a bounty on us."

Layla digested this news, but another implication assembled in her mind. "And you're planning to kill him – my uncle," she said.

"No, I'm not," Athena protested.

"I was," Sylvano admitted.

Athena gasped to hear him say it out loud. "Sylvano Rizio! You're a better man than that," she chastised him.

"No, I am not," Sylvano replied. Looking to Layla, he said. "I am a killer; I am nothing else. But I can't kill your uncle! What kind of man would I be, if I did to you what he did to me? But if I let him go – does that mean he wins? Revenge has been my whole life up to now. I don't know how to do anything else."

Sylvano's pain wrote itself on his face, despite his effort to contain it. He looked to each of his three friends in turn: Athena, then Wicklow, then Layla, upon whom his anguished gaze rested the longest. Layla broke her gaze away.

"I still don't understand," she said. "It's not that I don't believe you… he was always good to *me*."

"He taught me how to fire a musket, like a father," Sylvano said. "Doesn't change the fact that he's a kidnapper."

Wicklow, who had been quiet until that moment, said, "Everyone in the world has one face for the day and another for night. Dane had one face for the Movement, and another for everyone else. Even you, Layla. You've one for your uncle and another for us. How do *we* know which one is real?"

"What would you know of what I've had to do to survive?" Layla snapped at him.

"Hey!" Athena interjected, before Wicklow could answer. "Layla betrayed her own family to fight for *you* at the barricades, Wicklow. And today, she got us a ship. What more do you want from her? Moral purity?"

Wicklow glared at her, but did not answer.

"The way I see it," Athena continued, "The man who stole our lives is now paying for our journey to the Scatterlands. That's revenge enough for me. The only way he wins now, is by breaking our friendship. We win by staying friends. And if there's anything else in your hearts that demands satisfaction, demand it from the gods."

Her friends accepted this path by calming themselves. Layla opened her hand to Sylvano – a show of her love for him, as well as a plea to let go of his will to revenge.

Sylvano, understanding this, took a breath and took her hand.

Athena offered her hand to Wicklow. Reluctant and conflicted in his own way, he accepted.

Sylvano joined hands with Athena next, and Layla with Wicklow; and the circle was complete.

§ 30.

Wicklow paced from one end of the bridge to the other, pretending to be interested in the quality of its stonework, until Bailey arrived.

"I got the buyer waiting for you, down at the pub," Bailey said.

"Tell him it's not for sale anymore," Wicklow said.

"What?" Bailey chortled at him. "You can't do that. We had a deal."

"My situation's changed," Wicklow declared. "I'm going to the Scatterlands tomorrow. I need the map to get there."

Bailey shook his head in total disbelief. "They're going to find out you don't have the Knowledge. You said so yourself."

Wicklow nodded and said, "I'm going to have to learn it on the way."

"You're insane," Bailey declared.

"Tell your man he can buy the map when I return," Bailey promised. "In four months, at the latest. But not today."

Bailey shook his head. "We had a deal," he repeated, and walked away.

§ 31.

They arrived at the *Sun Dog*, moored at its berth in one of the city's canals. It was a two-masted schooner, twenty-four meters long, with one lower deck. Its hull was painted black, and its gunnels, rails, and ornaments in gold and crimson. Colonel Crave's men were at work, carrying barrels, sacks, coils of rope, and crates of provisions.

"Captain on deck!" shouted a voice as soon as Layla's heels touched the boards. The workers paused and turned to see who their captain was.

"Carry on, everyone," said Layla, grinning. To her friends she said, "Look at that – I just gave my first order as captain!"

Etienne d'Orsonnes stepped forward and saluted Layla. "Lady Darvi! May I introduce myself. Lieutenant Etienne d'Orsonnes. By the good graces of your uncle, Colonel Patroclus Crave, I am the first mate of the *Sun Dog*. Ship and crew are at your disposal." Acknowledging Sylvano, Wicklow, and Athena, he said, "Interesting company you keep."

Layla recovered from the surprise as quickly as she could. "First mate? That means you take my orders, yes?"

"Indeed, it does, my lady," said Etienne.

"Then my next order for you," she told him, "Is that my friends here are not to be harmed. Not by you, nor by any of the crew."

"Aye, captain," said Etienne, saluting her. "We are on your uncle's payroll now. And he ordered us to follow your orders. We are a loyal and – ha ha – *gentlemanly* crew."

Sylvano understood what Etienne was telling him.

Etienne smiled at Athena as she crossed the gangway and boarded the ship. "A pleasure to cross swords with you again, miss Kildare," he said, tipping his hat to her. "And you, mister... Carpinetto, was it?"

Sylvano made a weary smile.

Athena thought Etienne smiled like a butcher receiving a prize-winning steer into his abattoir. "Monsieur d'Orsonnes," she said, acknowledging him and keeping her feelings hidden.

"And you must be our esteemed Navigator," Etienne said to Wicklow.

"I am," Wicklow confirmed.

Etienne eyed him from head to foot, and said, "I have complete and total confidence in your expert experience."

Wicklow paused and decided the only reply which wouldn't start a fight was to say, "Thank you."

Layla moved to Etienne's side. "How soon until we're fully stocked and ready to fly?" she asked.

"Within the hour," Etienne reported.

"Come find me when you're ready to cast off."

Etienne acknowledged her words with a casual salute, and returned to his crew. "Right, you heard the lady! Pick up the pace! And don't touch her friends – these landlubbers are extra sensitive!"

Amid the laughter of the crew, Wicklow put everyone's worries into words: "We cannot trust this crew. Just this week, some of them were trying to kill us," he whispered to his friends.

"We also can't fly this ship without them," said Layla.

"They're *mercenaries*," Wicklow reminded them. "Their only loyalty is to money."

"Then we have to hope my uncle was the highest bidder," said Layla. "They don't get paid unless I come home safe."

"Great news for the rest of us," Sylvano said, grinning.

"You still sure you want to do this?" Wicklow asked Athena.

The leader of the outlaws surveyed the scene. The *Sun Dog's* crew appeared comfortable and experienced with the rigging, and happy to be sailing again. Like Wicklow, Athena too worried about where their loyalties might belong. But in her mind, this led to the final reason she believed the journey to Dawnland could not wait any longer.

"This world makes no sense to me anymore," she said. "We can stay here and fight one tyrant-king after another without ever getting anywhere. Or we can demand from the gods an explanation. We might never get another chance as good as this."

Sylvano placed a comforting hand on her shoulder.

"Let me show you how to make a sky-ship fly," said Layla.

§ 32.

In a room below the deck of the *Sun Dog*, Layla showed her friends a device that resembled a spherical kitchen range inside a matching metal cage. A series of metal rods and pipes extended out from the cage, through the walls and the floor, and toward the stern.

"This is the most wonderful thing ever made by anyone's hands: an *ethereal dynamo*," Layla explained.

"How does it work?" asked Sylvano.

"I've actually no idea!" Layla admitted, smiling. "All I know is that when you light a fire in it, the ship rises up in the air, and a strong tailwind rises with it."

A bell rang on the top deck. The four adventurers climbed the narrow stairs, almost as vertical as a ladder, to find out what was happening.

"Ready to cast off, my lady!" said Etienne.

"Last chance to talk us out of it," Wicklow said to Athena.

"Last chance to get cold feet," Athena ribbed him back. They traded friendly punches to each other's shoulders.

But when Athena wasn't looking, Wicklow made a melancholic face.

On deck, Athena turned to face the east. The green and tree-dressed north shore of the Heartwater sloped down to the water, and the south shore dimmed and faded in the distance. Between them, the water touched the sky. Dawnland seemed waiting for her, beyond the horizon. She could almost see it in her mind's eye.

She turned to Layla, the ostensible captain, and said "Time to fly."

Without hesitation, Layla gave the order. "Pull up the gangway, release the moorings, and set sails!"

"Our heading, my lady?" Etienne asked.

"Into the sunrise, to Dawnland," Layla said.

Etienne grinned, giving the impression he was prepared for that destination. "East, it is!"

He mingled with the crew, giving the specific orders for each sail, pulley, and station. The ship heaved itself down the canal, slow but heavy, pushed on by the barge poles of crewmembers and longshoremen. Once it maneuvered into the open water, the crew raised the sails. The ship lurched forward, into the wide and wine-dark Heartwater.

The four friends gathered on the prow for the best view of the path ahead. Their smiles were bright and excited, though also nervous.

When the ship sailed clear of the other ships coming and going from the city, Layla faced the crew on deck. "Fire up the dynamo! Take us to the sky!" she ordered.

"Aye, lady, aye!" Etienne acknowledged. With a whistle, he picked two crewmembers to follow him below deck. A moment later, wood-smoke rose from the dynamo's chimney. The wind came round to the stern and strengthened whereas the noise of the breakwater under the bow dimmed and ended. Only the gull-cries, the flapping of the canvas sails, and the small waves on the shoreline remained. The deck heaved and listed, first to port, then to starboard, then to port again. It steadied itself as it rose higher, level with the towers of the city behind them, and onward higher still.

"We're flying," Athena cried, delighted. "Actually flying!"

The friends laughed together and hugged each other; flying had made them children again.

On a rock on the edge of the water, far below the *Sun Dog*, Dubhdarra sat and watched them fly.

It seems you chose well, when you chose her.

The ageless voice drifted into Dubhdarra's hearing, from above and around him.

"You believe in her now?" the ranger asked.

We believe in what you're trying to do.

Dubhdarra grinned and laughed.

§ 33.

As he crossed the threshold of the coffee house, Bailey pulled his hood lower over his head, hoping that fewer people would notice his green skin, and none would see the leaves and twigs growing in his hair. He looked around the dining room and saw a mix of lawyers, accountants, professors, and middle-ranking military men crowded the tables, along with their companions and escorts. His weather-worn cloak and cracked leather boots made a sharp contrast with everyone else's silk coats, white wigs, and high heels. The rich scent of the coffee beans roasting on their hot plates made him thirsty.

Ignoring the annoyed stares from some of the coffee-drinkers, Bailey sat himself by a table across from a woman wearing a long blue coat and a white bandana.

"Bailey, is that right? You did hear that all the fringers were expelled from the city, after that festival of yours made so much noise," Dane Blackwood told him.

Bailey thought the best way to respond to that remark was to ignore it. "How would you like to make a very large pile of money?" he asked.

Dane gave him an ireful glare, then burst into loud laughter. "Oh Bailey, you're my favourite," she condescended him.

"I know who stole the map from your boss, and I know where they're taking it," Bailey said.

"You're desperate," Dane told him.

"Yes," Bailey admitted. "I have to leave my home before sundown, and I've nowhere to go. But if you gave me, let's say, a hundred crowns –"

"Fuck off," Dane said.

"Then I'd tell you about a ship with two army deserters on board, whose bounties you can collect. And an *astron* who doesn't know his left from his right – a bounty's on *his* head, too, by the way. And they're going straight to the place in the Scatterlands that made the Darvi clan rich. All you have to do is follow them."

Now Dane took Bailey seriously. "What ship?"

"That's the hundred-crown question, isn't it?" Bailey answered, smiling.

Dane sneered at him but dropped the coin-purse on the table anyway.

Bailey grinned all the wider and reached for the coins.

Dane pulled the purse back and said, "You're also coming *with* me."

Third Light: The Scatterlands

§ 34.

Athena scouted the capes and headlands before them with a spyglass. She gave each of her friends a turn to do the same. Sylvano used his turn to look back to Port Vivaldi.

"A shame we did not see the city in better times," he said.

"When we get back, I'll take you to the opera," Layla promised him. "And then after that, we'll tour the best salons. My favourite is the one for the philosophers, hosted by the countess d'Eclaireuse. They have the strangest ideas about everything, simply everything – it's a real brain-swim to hear them! And I know the most darling coffeehouse in the Piazza Dell'Alchimista, with frescoes on the ceiling painted by the great Estelle Trembley – the last she made before she ascended into heaven."

Something caught Athena's attention. "Looks like another schooner set sail just after us," she said.

"Probably just a local trader," said Layla.

"They're taking to the sky," Athena reported. "I think they're following us."

Her friends saw her report was correct... a second schooner climbed out of the water and matched their ascent.

Layla borrowed Athena's spyglass. The *Sun Dog*, having launched into the air first, gave her an angle to see the second ship's top deck. Standing at its prow, looking back with a spyglass of her own, was a woman with a white bandana. Beside her stood a man whose green hair fluttered in the wind like leaves on a tree.

"It's Dane," Layla said. She frowned. "Monsieur d'Orsonnes!"

The first mate's head appeared from one of the deck portals. "Aye, my lady?"

"Deploy side-sails."

"Already?" Etienne said, puzzled and annoyed. "We haven't even cleared the clouds!"

"It's either that, or ready the cannons," Layla told her, pointing at the ship who followed them.

Etienne saw it and smiled discretely. He directed the crew as they opened two long arms on either side of the ship, secured them to their deck fastenings, and unfolded the sails that hung from them. The lower corner of the side sails were pulled down into position by a cable that ran under the outer hull and up the other side of the ship. Sailors on the starboard side fastened the lower port-side sail; sailors on the port secured the lower starboard one. A sailor also climbed over each side of the hull on a rope ladder to place a wedge in the hinge of the side-sail mast, so that it would not swing back into the hull. He was secured by a safety harness and cable that his mates above held for him, and he made a show of enjoying the danger. The operation took mere minutes and this crew, Athena marvelled, were real experts. They raised the side-sails in full, using ropes that ran up the main sail, over a pulley, and down to the deck again. The ship lurched ahead as it caught more wind.

Athena checked the distance between her and the pursuer. With the extra sails on her ship, the distance between the two ships grew. However, Dane's ship deployed its own side-sails to match their speed.

"It isn't the ship or the armaments that will win this race," Athena surmised aloud to her friends. "It's the crew with the greater skill."

Athena touched the winged rabbit figurine. She didn’t trust her own crew, and considered whether she might need to call for Dubhdarra again.

"Monsieur d'Orsonnes!" said Athena. "Can you get us up into the clouds before that other ship comes close enough to fire on us?"

"Not likely," said the officer. "We're already under full sail." To Layla, he asked, "Shall I ready our cannons?"

Layla said, "Do it."

Etienne grinned. He strode down the deck and gave the order to the crew to prepare the cannons. They rolled out a pair of small four-pounders and brought up the gunpowder sacks and the cannonballs.

Athena realized that something else was wrong. She ran to the aft, just as the gunners were ready to load the gunpowder into the weapons. "Hold, hold!" she implored them.

The crew looked around each other, and to Etienne, wondering whether to obey.

"If we shoot first, we will start a fight we can't win," she said.

Etienne moved toward her, making a deliberate hard clunk with his boots with each step. "I believe the lady Darvi is the captain here," he said, challenging her authority.

Layla joined them. "What's happening?"

"We were enjoying a friendly discussion about who wears the heels on this ship," said d'Orsonnes, grinning again.

"If we fire on them," Athena said, "they will destroy us!"

"If we fire *first*," d'Orsonnes countered, "and hit them in just the right place, they won't fire back. We'll be clear all the way to Dawnland."

"Sylvano, you've got gunnery training?" Athena asked.

"I do," her friend replied.

"How soon until that ship comes close enough to fire on us?"

Etienne interrupted before Sylvano could reply. "They'll be in range before we can hide in the clouds."

"That's because they're in range already," Sylvano said.

Etienne grinned. "I told you no lies," he smirked. Returning to the gun crews, he said, "All right, boys. You know what to do."

The gun crews had the cannons loaded and ready. One of them brought the smouldering wick to its detonation key. But Athena still thought something was wrong with the way Etienne gave his last order.

"If they've been in range all this time," Athena asked, "why didn't they fire first?" Athena asked.

Seeing that Layla found Athena's question reasonable, Etienne stepped between the two women, separating them. "They've not fired yet because they want to get closer, strafe us with buckshot, and then board us," he growled. Turning to Layla, who he knew was listening, he said, "Take it from someone who got his sky-legs before you were born. If we fire first, we put them off the chase. We don't even need to sink them to do it. It'll be enough to damage the bow. But if we stand here arguing about it, they'll commandeer us without resistance. They'll take your friends home to collect the bounties on their heads. And as for you, captain, your uncle won't be able to rescue you from where they will take you, I promise you that!"

"Are we in range to take out their masts?" Layla asked.

"My boys know exactly where to take aim," Etienne said, grinning again.

His words gave Athena another chill. "Sylvano, Wicklow, with me," she said. She dashed down the step-stairs to the deck below and ran into the chamber that held the ethereal dynamo. The fire was up and burning in its heart and the two wheels on either side of it spun in opposite directions imparting a colourful glow to the air around it.

"Let's fill this with more fuel," Athena said, as she cut open a sack of gunpowder. "Maybe we *can outrun* that other ship!"

"But what if Etienne was right, and they try to board us unless we fire first?" Sylvano said.

"Did you hear what Etienne said up there?", Athena asked. "He said 'my boys know where to take aim'. When they fire, they will miss *on purpose*."

Believing that Athena was right, Wicklow and Sylvano helped her dump more kindling into the ethereal dynamo. The fire burned hotter; the wheels spun faster. In almost the same moment, they felt the ship lurch ahead.

"Now hang on to something," said Athena. She ran back to the top deck and made for the ship's helm. A lever beside the wheel controlled the angle by which the ship rose up or sank down in the air. She pushed the helmsman away, and pulled the lever all the way back, tilting the ship's prow up to the sky.

"Too far, too far!" Etienne yelled at her. In the time it took for him to cross the deck and reach the helm, she realized he might be right – the ship was tilting far enough that things were sliding across the deck and piling up on the railing by the aft. She pushed the lever forward, hoping that the ship would come to a safer angle.

Etienne aimed his wheel-lock at her. "Get off the helm, kid," he ordered her.

Layla joined him. "What the hell are you doing, Athena!" she demanded.

"We can't fight them," Athena said. "But we might be able to out-fly them."

Etienne snapped his fingers – his men recognized the order to draw their own weapons and aim them at Athena. "Off my helm, Kildare! Next time, it'll be my pistol doing the asking."

Athena chanced a look over her shoulder. Dane's ship was further behind them again, but still committed to the race.

Sylvano rushed to stand between Athena and Etienne and raised his musket. "They will be your last words in this life, I swear to you!" he threatened.

Etienne laughed at him. "You've got spirit, boy. But no sense to go with it. Look around you!"

Sylvano looked. A dozen sailors had their swords or guns drawn, ready at Etienne's orders to take the helm from Athena. And Layla, in principle the captain and therefore the one who could break the standoff by giving new orders, had crouched down on the deck and grabbed a railing, fearful of falling off the ship. She looked back and forth between Athena at the helm, and Blackwood's ship behind them.

Athena said to Wicklow, "If you have as much pull with clouds as you do with water, maybe you could do something?"

"Like what?" Wicklow said.

"I don't know... bring the clouds down to us?"

Wicklow saw that, with Athena and Sylvano holding off Etienne and his men, and with Layla possessed by indecision, he might be the only person who could act. He ran to the prow to stand on the railing. With a hand gripping a bowsprit cable for balance, he recited an incantation in an ancient lost language.

The ceiling of clouds thickened and darkened. The wind picked up and buffeted both ships from several directions. Ropes and cables rattled against each other, and strained against their moorings. Then the nearest, largest, cloud seemed to spread down and out and poured out its rain.

Athena understood what Wicklow was doing. She angled the ship to fly straight into the downpour, and then upward again into the heart of the cloud.

"And how do you expect to get anywhere if you can't see where you're going?" Etienne growled at her.

"I expect *they* won't see where we're going either," she replied, as she turned the ship to starboard, then righted it again.

The *Sun Dog* was now enveloped in the cloud. With no sea below, no shore to the side, and no sun above to give anyone their bearings, Athena felt they had entered another world. It seemed a space almost larger than the ship itself, with the barest gradients of grey in their surroundings. Only the occasional flapping of the sails, and the occasional glint of a Whisperlight, suggested they were still moving at all.

"Now, quiet!" Athena ordered.

Etienne shook his head. "Enough of this amateurism. Gun crews, prepare to fire!" he ordered.

"Quiet!" Athena repeated. "They can't see us, but they might still *hear* us."

"Widest spread. Maybe something will hit them," Etienne ordered, ignoring Athena. "Ready! And –"

"Hold!" said Layla, standing up.

All eyes turned to her.

"Hold, and quiet," Layla repeated. "We're out of danger now. If we fire on them, they'll know where we are."

Etienne shook his head, disappointed. He lowered his weapon and signalled for his men to do the same.

Athena closed her eyes and let her shoulders drop in relief.

The boom of a cannon filled the air – Dane's ship had fired. The zing of a score of small bullets flew by, leaving a trail of whirls and spirals in its path through the cloud. But it missed the *Sun Dog* by a wide margin.

"Buckshot," said Etienne. "I told you they want to board us."

"Quiet!" Layla hissed, seeing as the gun crews were anxious to return fire.

A second cannon-shot exploded out, but quieter. The tracks of its ordinance passed through the clouds further away. More of the crew relaxed; Athena's strategy of hiding in the clouds was saving their lives.

A third cannon-shot was quieter still, and more distant. Its origin seemed hard to grasp; the sound came from all directions at once. No one saw the buckshot trails in the clouds. Their enemy had lost them.

Etienne glared at Athena, pleased to be still alive, but annoyed that it was her strategy, and not his, which had saved their lives.

"Steady on, and keep everyone quiet, Monsieur d'Orsonnes," Layla ordered him. "Athena, may I have a word?"

They retreated to the prow of the ship, where they could speak more privately.

"What the hell did you think you were doing, giving orders to my crew like that!" Layla hissed at Athena.

"Then why did you do *nothing*?" Athena whispered back.

The fire in Layla's demeanour extinguished. She collapsed on a bench. "You're right. I was pretty useless back there, wasn't I?"

"Well, you know," said Athena, not needing to say anything more.

"So," Layla said, "where do we go from here?"

"I don't know yet," Athena admitted. "I suppose that when we get to Dawnland, we can –"

"What do you mean, you don't know?" Layla said, some of her fire returning. "I got this ship for you because I believed you knew what you were doing!"

Athena, taken aback, said, "I *do* know what I'm doing, but how could I have planned for your uncle hiring a bevy of street thugs to fly the ship?"

Perched near the foremast, Etienne took in the gist of the conversation. He smiled.

Layla said to Athena, "I'm talking about Dawnland. Do you have a plan for what to do when we get there?"

"We follow the Whisperlights."

"What if we don't find any?"

"We have four months to find them," Athena said, with confidence. "That should be more than enough time."

Etienne d'Orsonnes approached, hands open, smiling – the perfect picture of a loyal first officer. "I think we're far enough away from our chaperone now," he said. "So, what are your orders?"

Layla looked to Athena; a glance that Etienne noticed. He smirked upon seeing it.

"Dawnland," said Layla. "We sail for Dawnland."

"Aye, lady, aye," Etienne said, smiling as he left to convey the orders to the crew. "South by south-east, and full sail ahead!"

Athena could tell by his face that he had formed a new picture in his mind of who was in command of the ship.

Layla saw it too. "I hope you have a plan for what to do when your luck runs out," she said to Athena.

Her words caused some of the blood to drain out of Athena's limbs. She sat down and looked into the surrounding fog.

§ 35.

"I think you all know why I called you to this meeting," Layla said to Sylvano and Wicklow, her voice low to avoid eavesdroppers. "And I think you know why I didn't invite Athena."

"That first mate of yours will kill us and take the ship for himself, the first chance he gets," Sylvano said.

"He knows he won't get paid unless I make it home alive," Layla said. "Having said that… if we come across anything that's worth *more* than what my uncle's paying him, he'll lock you up and sell you to bounty hunters. And he'll hold me for ransom. We need a plan, for what to do when he makes his move, and we can't let Athena know about it."

"But we *have* to tell her – she's in danger too," said Wicklow.

"No, Layla's right," said Sylvano. "If we tell her, she'll do something on her own, without warning. I've known her since we were kids. When she makes up her mind about something, she doesn't listen to anybody."

"The most important thing," said Layla, "is that this crew has to understand that I'm the captain. I give the orders – not Monsieur d'Orsonnes. And, *when* I give orders, I want one of you on hand to make sure that they are obeyed."

"I am your most worshipful and obedient servant, my dear lady," said Sylvano, as he reached for Layla's hand to kiss.

Layla rolled her eyes. "It can't be in jest, Sylvano," she reminded him. "Our lives might depend on it."

"Of course," said Sylvano.

Wicklow said, "We should also stay together. No one lets another of us go anywhere alone. And at least one of us has eyes on Etienne d'Orsonnes at all times."

"That will be hard to do," said Layla. "He sleeps in the aft storeroom by himself, with the door closed."

"Maybe we can lock him in there?" Sylvano suggested.

"If we do that," said Wicklow, "the crew will mutiny right away."

"But we have to do *something*," said Sylvano. "And soon… before *they* do something first."

The three sat in silence for an uncomfortable moment.

"I think," said Layla, "we may have to… you know… find a way to –"

"I think you're probably right," Sylvano agreed, sparing her the need to say it out loud.

"Is there *no* other choice?" Wicklow wondered.

Another uncomfortable moment passed.

Layla shrugged and sighed. "I don't like it but I can't see any other way."

"I don't like it either," said Wicklow.

Sylvano said, "I used to be a soldier. Hurting people was kind of my job. But this… there's no honour in it. No *virtue*. There's only –"

"Don't say it," Layla interrupted him. "If you put a name on it, you'll make it real. Best if we just do it, then find a way to make peace with it in our hearts."

Yet another uncomfortable moment passed.

"It's settled, then," Layla declared.

Wicklow nodded, agreeing with her. Sylvano did not move.

"So, how do we do it?" Wicklow asked.

"Sylvano, you're the soldier," Layla said.

"But I was a sniper, not an assassin," Sylvano said.

"You must have trained for close quarters," Layla suggested.

"I did," he confirmed.

"So, what's the best way?"

Sylvano breathed deep as he considered a few possibilities. "Best if you do it at night, during third watch, when everyone on board is asleep.

One person covers his mouth, from behind. A second person comes in front and –" He made a stabbing gesture, unable to put the action into words.

"Then, I suppose we'll have to throw him – his body – overboard," Wicklow said. "And pray that no one sees us do it."

"Your job then," Layla told him, "Is to keep Athena distracted. You're the Navigator and we can't risk any harm coming to you."

Wicklow nodded and looked away.

They rose to leave the cabin without saying anything more, but they traded dark looks among each other, to prepare themselves for what they had resolved to do.

Wicklow was the last to leave.

§ 36.

The clouds cleared by eventide, creating a gold, red, and purple sunset behind them, and ahead a horizon of deep blue, fading almost to black. The first star of the night announced itself in the corner of Athena's eye, as though it had always been there. One by one, and in the same way, more stars came to be, until by the middle of the first night-watch when the whole sky glimmered with them. When the ship's bell marked the start of the second watch, the milky-dim glow of the Night Road emerged from the horizon off the port bow, arced to the east overhead, and touched the distance again off the starboard stern, like a great celestial portal opening into the unknown.

Athena always volunteered for the third watch, the one that took the ship from the darkness to the dawn. She wanted to be the first to see the sunrise, and the first to sight its place on the horizon along the line from the main mast to the bowsprit, so she could assure herself the *Sun Dog* still flew in the right direction. Her friends took turns joining her.

By the evening of the third day after they left the sight of land, the ship passed among a cluster of islands that were more like the summits of great rocky pillars rising from the sea. The shore of each was a sheer vertical cliff, denying a safe harbour to any waterborne ships that might sail here.

"The Wardens of the East," Monsieur d'Orsonnes said they were called.

"Last outpost of old Summerland, before the Scatterlands begin."

Seabirds of all kinds nested among the shrubs and vines that clung to the crags and ledges, including many whom Athena had never seen before. Their quacking and gobbling echoed on the neighbouring islands, almost as loud as the waves crashing on the cliffs below. Athena saw a trio of birds watching the ship fly by – each bird was half as tall as Athena herself, their feathers were red and gold, and they scattered glowing sparks on the nearby ground whenever they fluttered their wings. One of them launched into the air, passed over the deck of the *Sun Dog* twice, and nesting again on another ledge, a small trail of flame followed him where he flew.

Etienne d'Orsonnes took aim with his musket and shot one of them. Its feathers set the twigs and mosses around it on fire where it fell. He laughed.

"What did you do that for!" Athena scolded him.

Etienne grinned. "An old tradition. Keeping mother nature in line," he said.

Athena could only gaze aghast as Etienne shot two more of them, laughing to himself all the while.

As the edge of the sun sank behind the Wardens, Etienne said, "That was the last landmark of the known world. We're in the hands of your Navigator, now. Or else, in the hands of the gods."

A blue-black shroud rolled up from the east and covered the sky with night-time.

Wicklow gazed into it and shuddered.

§ 37.

Wicklow sat near the ship's prow, holding the map open before him. He compared its stars to those which shimmered in the sky above and measured the differences with a small collection of geometry tools.

"So, this is what Navigators do?" Athena asked him, playfully.

"If you hold the map up like this..." Wicklow demonstrated for her as he spoke, "then you can line up the stars in the map with the stars in the sky. Then you measure the angle that you're holding it, relative to the ship's heading, to know whether we have to steer right or left to get back in line. But there's a problem."

"Yes?"

"Too many clouds tonight," Wicklow said, grinning.

Athena laughed. "Maybe you can banish them for us," she suggested.

Wicklow looked back to the deck. All was quiet and still save for the sails that rippled in the moderate breeze. The lamps hanging from the masts made little pools of warm light beneath them. And a dark figure stole across the deck, from the forward hatch to the stern hatch, careful to avoid the lamp-light pools and any of the deck-boards that creaked. By the silhouette and the gait, Wicklow gathered it was Sylvano, on his way to Etienne's berth in the aft storeroom.

"The *real* problem is that holding the map by hand isn't precise enough," Wicklow said, keeping Athena's attention on him instead of on the deck behind him. "It doesn't take account of the passage of time… the distance on the calendar from today to Midsummer at midnight. You'd need a sextant the size of the mast, an abacus with a hundred beads, and a whole day to do all the math. Navigators do it all in their heads, in only a few minutes. We don't need any of the tools. Some of us don't even need the maps."

"I've often wondered why it is that only *astrons* can be Navigators," Athena said.

"We ourselves wonder that," Wicklow informed her, with a small sardonic smile. "I once heard a story, though. We came to Summerland from some other place in the Cosmos. Some other star, up there… nobody knows which one. They say though, that some kind of slow-moving catastrophe had come to our world. The gods brought us to Summerland to save our lives."

Athena considered the dim golden glow in Wicklow's eyes; something no other people in Summerland possessed, as far as she knew. It seemed like a sign that the story had to be true.

Behind them, another shadow slinked across the deck – the second member of the conspiracy against Etienne. Wicklow glanced at it, and hoped Athena wouldn't notice it.

"What is it?" Athena asked, sensing his distraction.

"It takes ten years to finish your apprenticeship as a Navigator," Wicklow said. "Some people take longer."

Wicklow glanced back across the deck when he thought Athena wasn't looking at him. The ship was as still as ever at night with the occasional flap of a sail, and the groan of the lumber where the ropes fastened the masts to the hull. But he imagined the possible scene below, where Layla and Sylvano gathered outside Etienne's door, with daggers drawn.

"In the first two years, it's all math and logic puzzles, with some physical training," Wicklow continued. "After that, they add science, poetry, music, philosophy… though I'm not sure why. We do this while on the road, too; we are a nomadic people."

"Sounds gruelling," Athena said.

"In the final test, you go to the Whisperlights," Wicklow said. "Some of us never make it that far."

Athena nodded. "I've been wondering about them, too," she said. "Dubhdarra said the world was supposed to be beautiful. Maybe the whispers are part of that. But everybody's afraid of them."

Wicklow turned to meet Athena's eyes. "Athena, you see…" he said, preparing himself to reveal his secret.

"Hey, look at that!" Athena interrupted. She pointed to a dark patch on the horizon ahead. It was black against the dark navy-blue of sea and sky.

"Is that… Dawnland?" she asked.

Wicklow strained his eyes to see better. The line of darkness seemed framed on its top by the peaks of hills and knolls.

"It's *land*, anyway!" he said. Sensing an opportunity, he rang the ship's bell and shouted, "Land ho! Land ho!"

Within a few heartbeats, the crew poured out of the hatches, still in their undershirts and stockings. They leaned on the railing and studied the darkness. "Dawnland!" they said. "But it's so small!", and "How do you know how big Dawnland is?" Several repeated the old proverb that

Athena had heard before... "It's the Scatterlands – you can't land in the same place twice."

Layla and Sylvano joined the crew to see the sight for themselves. Wicklow exchanged a glance with Layla... a raised eyebrow and a pensive breath, to ask if the deed had been done. Layla shook her head. So, the answer was *no*. Wicklow closed his eyes. Reprieved.

At last, Etienne d'Orsonnes rose from the hatch, with his coat and boots on, and a spyglass in his hand.

"It's only the first rock of the Scatterlands," he called it. "Didn't expect to see one so soon."

"So, it's not Dawnland?" Athena asked him.

"Dawnland is no rock in the ocean. It's a continent, nearly half the size of Summerland itself," Etienne explained. "Not that it *looks* the same every time you find it. But we can come ashore *here*, if you like. Replenish water, and wood for the dynamo. See if there's anything else of value. This expedition won't pay for itself!"

Athena sensed Etienne was willing to take orders from her, and was encouraging her to give the orders, for some complex reason of his own. But she also knew the scandal she would create between her friends if she did so.

"Layla?" she said, to let it be seen that the captain gives the orders.

"Take her in," Layla said.

"Aye, lady, aye," Etienne said, though he glanced at Athena as he spoke. Then he grabbed some of the crew by the shoulders and pushed them to work. "Gentlemen! Take in the side-sails. Helm, come down to sea-level. Douse the dynamo. Prepare the shore-boats. Prepare to drop the anchor. Come on, lads – ten lashes for anyone still picking their nose by the time the ship hits the water!"

The ship drifted down and splashed into the ocean with a lurch that threw some of the crew off their feet.

Athena and her friends came together on the bow to watch the approach. Layla, Wicklow, and Sylvano held back for a moment, to speak low into each other's ears.

"Tomorrow, we try again," said Layla.

Wicklow nodded. "Tomorrow," he said.

§ 38.

The crew attempted to anchor the *Sun Dog* an arrow's flight from the shore. However, they found that even with the anchor chain unspooled to its full length, the ship still drifted.

"Strange," said Etienne, as he heard the report from the sailors as to the water depth. "It's as if the water's as deep as the ocean until three paces from the shore... that's the Scatterlands for you."

Layla said, "I want you to command the shore party."

"Begging your pardon, my lady," said Etienne, "but as much as that's the normal custom, wouldn't you rather give the honour to one of your companions? Athena Kildare, perhaps. She's clever, and she's fearless. But she needs more experience. She could learn that here."

Layla sensed that Etienne had another reason for wanting to send Athena off the ship, but she had a reason of her own to send Etienne instead – one she couldn't tell him.

"Let her learn by following your example for a while," Layla said.

Etienne tipped his hat to her and returned to his usual duties.

Layla wasn't sure if his gesture was sincere, but she accepted it. When he was out of sight, she perked an eyebrow to Sylvano. He shrugged by way of reply.

With Athena at the rudder, and Etienne at the prow, the shore-boat came alongside the edge of the island. It was a crest of black and chitinous rock, arranged in close-knit hexagonal columns, each just wide enough to serve as a footstep. The crew clambered on to them, glad to touch solid ground for the first time in more than two weeks.

They tied the ship's cables to several knobby trees that rooted themselves in the thin grykes between some of the stones, higher up the cliff. The mass of the ship pulled the first two trees out of the ground, but the crew handled the next ones better, and soon made the ship secure.

"Looks like there's no fresh water here," Etienne said to Athena. "But there's plenty of seabirds, which means plenty of meat and eggs."

"My first step in the Scatterlands, and we're collecting eggs," Athena complained.

"On my first step in the Scatterlands," said Etienne, "the birds were so big, one of them swooped down and snatched up a mate of mine and flew away with him. Never saw the bugger again."

Athena decided she had it lucky. She took her musket-rifle and a basket and went hunting for seabirds.

Sylvano also took up a musket and a basket following a different route. It was one that shadowed Etienne, while trying not to appear that he was doing so.

"It would be a shame if Etienne slipped on one of these rocks, and fell into the sea," he said to Layla.

"These rocks are so slippery after a rain, aren't they?" she replied.

The crew of the shore-boat took turns bird hunting, and keeping a watch on the trees, lest the *Sun Dog* uproot its moorings again. The sun dropped down to a hand's width above the horizon, and faded into orange behind thin clouds.

Sylvano and Layla followed Etienne to the far side of the island – a short scramble over the stone columns and pillars, as the island was less than half a league across at its widest. They held back when Etienne sat on one of the columns, put up his feet on another, rested his back on a third, and lit up a smoking-pipe.

Sylvano cocked the hammer of his musket. "I think I can get him in one shot," he whispered.

Layla prepared her pistol. "If you miss and he charges us, I'll get him."

Sylvano rested the barrel of his musket on a rock to steady his aim. He closed one eye and lined up his shot. He moved his finger to the trigger.

Across the island, Athena found two crewmen cutting some trees to make a small campfire. They had a grill and a frying pan, and an albatross which they had already field-dressed for cooking.

"Share some of that with me, and I won't tell Etienne what you're doing," she offered.

They accepted. When they got the kindling lit and fanned the flames to ignite the larger logs, Athena noticed that the rock on which they built the fire was not like the rest of the island. It was weather-beaten, far smoother, and it extended into a peninsula almost as long as the rest of the island. As the fire grew, the rock rumbled and groaned – waters along the shore swirled and crashed into heavier waves. Then the peninsula raised itself up, and crashed into the sea again, spraying water all around. The island itself listed slightly, turned, and moved. As Athena struggled to keep her footing, she noticed that a rocky bulge near the end of the peninsula was not a rock at all. but the lid of a great reptilian eye. It opened and swirled around, looking back at her.

"This isn't an island," she told herself, to make the discovery real. "Quick, put that fire out! Everyone – back to the ship!" she ordered the crew.

Seeing the waters creep higher on the island's shore, the two sailors dropped everything and ran back to the shore-boat.

Etienne jumped up as a wave splashed close to his feet and almost pulled him out to sea.

Sylvano and Layla ducked down, lest Etienne might see them.

"By the gods, the island is sinking!" Layla cried.

Athena heard that as she ran by. "It's not an island!" she told them. "It's a sea creature! Back to the ship!"

Skidding, clamouring, and sometimes tripping on the rocks – the creature's scales – the crew cut the mooring cables and threw themselves into the shore-boat.

When they reached the *Sun Dog*, Athena looked back to see two members of the crew stranded on the sea-turtle's back, frozen in terror. Only a thin ridge of the colossal creature's back remained, surrounded by a swath of churning and crashing water, rushing in to take the turtle's place.

"Jump in! Jump in!" Athena shouted at them. To the other sailors on the shore-boat, she ordered, "Turn around - we have to help them!"

But Etienne howled "Belay that order!", and the sailors obeyed.

As Athena watched, the water swallowed the two men as the turtle disappeared beneath them. The backwash ensured they would never come to the surface again.

Etienne extended a hand to Athena to help her out of the shore-boat. She accepted a hand from Sylvano instead.

"We could have saved them!" she howled at Etienne.

"If we had turned around, the water would have swallowed us, and we all would have died," Etienne told her.

Athena looked to the swirling froth that lay on the surface of the sea, in the place where two men died. "I suppose you're right," she admitted.

"The ship comes first, before any of us," Etienne reminded her. "Every man who sets foot on these planks knows it. You want to be a leader? You need to know it, too."

He walked away, passing by an astonished Layla as he went, and giving her a cursory nod on the way; enough to tell her that she, too, needed to learn that lesson.

Layla stopped him. "You *knew* that wasn't an island, didn't you?" she accused. "You *wanted* Athena to make a mistake. And you wanted the crew to see it!"

"What I want, my lady," said Etienne, "is for the mission to succeed, and the *Sun Dog* to be commanded by her rightful captain."

"My mission - my captaincy!" Layla said, quiet but insistent.

Etienne only grinned and doffed his hat for her. "As you say, my lady," he grinned.

He walked away, and Layla could not think of a reply to stop him.

§ 39.

The *Sun Dog* found good tailwinds and clear skies the next day. The crew took time for games with cards and dice, which Sylvano sometimes joined. Athena used the fair weather to learn how to handle the helm.

"On a sky-ship," Layla explained to her, "we don't use the rudder to steer. We use the *tail*."

"What's that?" Athena asked.

Layla pointed to an array of metal fins that fanned out from the stern of the ship. "That's the tail," she said. "They're attached to the dynamo, which attracts the wind. With this wheel, you can point them in the direction where you want the wind to come from. Try it!"

Athena turned the ship's wheel. The effort required some strength, for she was controlling a complex arrangement of pulleys and gears. Though the tailfins were well balanced, they were also heavy. Soon she felt the wind tussle her hair from a different direction, and she heard the change in the flapping of the sails. The line along the ship's axis, from the two masts to the tip of the bow, soon pointed at a new position on the horizon.

"That's the easy part," Layla said. "The hard part is figuring when the dynamo might burn low. First, you'll notice the wind coming from other directions when you haven't moved the wheel. Next, you'll notice we lose altitude. If we fall too fast... well, I don't need to tell you what will happen."

"I can well imagine!" Athena said with a worried laugh.

Wicklow taught Layla to use the compass and the sextant. She shot the sun to get the ship's latitude and surprised everyone by calculating the ship's latitude in her head.

"You're strange for a Navigator," Etienne said to Wicklow, observing them.

"How so?"

"Most Navigators I've worked with don't need a compass," he explained. "They know which way to go just by feeling it."

"I was taught a different way," the *astron* said. It was as near as he could get to the truth without giving away the fact that he was teaching himself as they flew.

Etienne smirked. "Well, I suppose there's as many ways to chart the Scatterlands as there are Navigators to do it," he said. "But between you, me, and the sea, I've never known it to take this long."

Wicklow acknowledged it with a resigned shrug. "That's the Scatterlands for you," he said.

Etienne smirked at the use of his own words from the past. He turned to Layla. "Captain, you should know the crew has been talking, and... they'd be grateful if you were to take a wee detour. Some place where we can replenish water. Maybe catch some fish and seabirds, or snare us some game."

"Supplies getting low?" Layla asked.

"Journey's taking longer than expected," Etienne said, with another smirk. "Now, on every other ship I've ever served, the best way to find such a place was always to find the Whisperlights." Nodding to Wicklow, he said, "You *astron_* have a sense for them, don't you? No need to answer; I know it's true."

Wicklow's discomfort showed in his glowering gaze and tightening muscles.

"The thing about the whispers," Etienne continued, "is you see them most of all around bogs, marshes, rivers, and lakes. Sometimes in forests. Well, they can live anywhere, of course. But that water – that's their home. So, the easiest way for us to refill the larder is for you to find the whispers. That can't be hard for you, eh? No need for a compass or any fancy instruments at all."

"I'll talk to the captain," Wicklow said, controlling the tone of his voice with care.

"That's all I'm asking," Etienne said. He walked away, tipping his hat, and leaving Wicklow with a terrible suspicion that Etienne knew his secret now. He took his place on the Navigator's seat, near the ship's wheel, and willed himself to the task.

By evening, he had given the ship's pilot no new course to take. Layla heard the crew whispering about it and growing restless.

"You know, I'm beginning to think Etienne has a point." Layla said to Athena. "He's done nothing all day but stare at the map."

"I'm quite sure he can find the way," Athena replied. "I'm just not sure he *wants* to."

"How do you mean?" Layla asked.

"Best if you let him tell you himself," Athena suggested.

Athena, Layla, and Sylvano gathered around their friend at the Navigator's seat. "Wicklow, I gotta ask what you're doing," Layla said.

Wicklow looked up. "The Whisperlights are not the little love-pixies you think they are. They're monsters," he said.

"They taught me how to read the map," Athena reminded her friend.

"Aye," Wicklow said. "But what they *took* from me was too much!"

Athena was curious. "What did they take from you?" she asked.

Wicklow sighed. "My father," he admitted, at last. "Walked into a cloud of them once. It was the last stage of his training. No one ever saw him again."

"You're saying he got hired on a ship and never returned?" Layla asked.

"I'm saying he disappeared!" Wicklow snapped. "They do that to people, sometimes; didn't I warn you about them? And when they took him, I learned a very important lesson: that this world is made of chaos and craziness, and no one is ever going to stay by me for long. Imagine being fourteen years old and having to learn that."

"I can imagine being twelve," Sylvano drawled.

"Sylvano, please?" Athena chided him. "The man has just revealed his deepest fear to us."

"I don't fear them," Wicklow insisted. "But I know what they are. And I prefer to keep as much distance from them as I can."

Layla, however, drew a conclusion. "Didn't you tell me the other night that going *into* them is the last stage of a Navigator's training?"

With that question, Wicklow's face fell. He nodded to confirm, then bowed his head, defeated. His secret was out.

"Well, that's the ribbon to tie a bow on this perfect day," Sylvano said.

Athena looked to the sea and the horizon, and saw it was now trackless, endless, and eternal. Anything at all could dwell behind the clouds or upon the next island – anything but the way home. She clutched her hand over her heart.

Layla said, "We can't let Etienne find out. He'll take the ship. Wicklow, you *must* find them."

"I already know where they are," Wicklow said, his voice resigned. "I can always feel them."

"You don't have to go into them. We only need you to point the way," Layla said.

"And we'll stay by you, the whole time," Athena promised. "Don't be afraid."

Wicklow smirked at her. "Dubhdarra says it better," he said.

"That's true," Athena admitted. "But I'm still saying it."

Wicklow regarded her for a long moment. Then he pointed to the horizon. "That way," he said. "Bearing one-three-zero degrees."

His friends patted his shoulders and thanked him. Layla stepped away to deliver the new heading to the pilot.

When he and Athena were alone, Wicklow said, "Don't make me regret this."

§ 40.

Another day of smooth sailing on Wicklow's new heading brought the *Sun Dog* to another island. It was larger, more mountainous, and glowing a deep crimson in the sunset. As night advanced and the island turned dark, a blue-white glow curled across the waters of the shore, undulating with the waves, and spiralling around with the inscrutable currents below. The glow seemed to move, swim, and glitter with a life of its own.

"Whisperlights of the sea," Etienne named them. Athena smiled.

The crew berthed the ship in the water, drove stakes in the beach, and ran ropes to the ship to hold it in place. Athena picked up one of the beach pebbles. In her torchlight it was a translucent pinkish colour but changed to bluish as she turned it over in her hands. Sylvano picked up another of the pebbles to take a closer look.

"These could be valuable back home," said Sylvano. "Imagine carriage ornaments that change colour as you drive by."

Then the stone bit his finger.

Shrieking with surprise and disgust, he dropped it and backed away from the spot where it fell. Looking around, he noticed dozens of similar 'stones' scuttling around, chewing on strands of seaweed, and climbing up the sides of the shore boat. Some had climbed up the sides of the sailor's legs without their knowledge.

"Get them off, they'll sink the boat, get them off!" Sylvano ordered.

With his help, the panicked crew grabbed all the creatures they saw climbing into the shore-boat, threw them back on the beach, and pushed the boat back into the water. But other creatures climbed on to the cables and scrambled toward the ship. The crew scraped them off with their shovels.

Athena, however, had already wandered further inland. The beach gave way to a moist and mulchy soil, from which grew various reeds and tallgrasses. A scattering of palm trees grew further up the slope, whose trunks swelled and shrank and swelled again, as though they were breathing. They produced strange maroon-coloured, bulb-like flowers, some of which opened for her when she passed close by.

"Careful!" Sylvano warned. "If the stones bite, who knows what the flowers do."

Athena touched one of the flowers. It broke from its branch, and floated away into the air, carried by the light breeze. A few heartbeats later, it burst, spreading a cloud of pollen into the air. Some of it fell on Athena, where it sizzled on her armour and stung her skin. She went back to the water to wash it off.

"That's the Scatterlands for you," said Sylvano, grinning to see her in that state.

Athena splashed a handful of water on him, grinning.

"Shall we return to the ship? Find another island?" Sylvano suggested. "This one might be too dangerous."

"I don't think we can ask that of Wicklow again," Athena said. "Not for a while."

She gazed deeper into the island's interior. The low slope of the beach and the woodland rose higher to make hills of stone and sand. Something resembling an obelisk rose in the middle distance.

"We know there are Whisperlights here," said Athena. "We saw them in the water. So, we'll stay at least until tomorrow, to see if they come out at night. In the meanwhile, we explore. See if there's anything we can use to top up our supplies."

"Some of these men don't want to set foot on this island ever again," Sylvano informed her.

"Why? Are the men made of cheese? Do they think they'll be eaten by a mouse?" Athena said, loud enough for the men to hear. "I'm sure their friends back home would love to hear how *someone like me* had more courage." She traced her fingers on her chin and struck a pose.

Some of the men jabbed each other on the shoulders; Athena knew she had made her point.

They rowed down the coast of the island some more, and found a river mouth, flanked on either side of its banks by rows of fallen and crumbled obelisks. Strange purple birds with long legs and long necks stalked the reeds along the shoreline, hunting for fish. Long and fat green snakes swam across the water and the boat crew witnessed one of them catch and eat an eight-legged frog on a lily pad.

The river water was fresh, and boiling it would make it safe to drink. Layla ordered the crew to bring all the empty barrels and firkins from the ship and fill them with all the fresh water they could carry, and all the fish and birds they could catch. "We shall feast like kings tonight – but only if you're brave enough to sit on the beach with me to eat it!" she said.

The crew boasted of their bravery, as loud as Athena expected. She smiled, confident that they would return.

They cleared an area of the beach from the 'snappers' – the name they had decided to give to the little creatures that looked like stones but which bit like snapping turtles. They built a fire and roasted some of the birds and fish they had caught that day, and shared them out using palm fronds for plates. Some of the crew knocked the exploding flower-pods off the palm trees with long sticks, so they could tie up their hammocks between them. Others made a game of shooting them down with pistols and muskets, until Etienne ordered them to save their ammunition. Bottles of rum were shared and emptied, stories told of other times people had come to the Scatterlands, and the discoveries and battles and tragedies that followed.

Athena enjoyed the stories, but she gave them only half of her attention. The other half, she gave to the darkness between the trees.

"Looking for them?" Wicklow asked her.

"Strange that I haven't seen any yet," Athena said. "Something very *like* them is in the water, along the shore. I was sure we'd see them over the fields. But instead, there's... well, it's gone now."

"What?"

"I *thought* it was a Whisperlight alone, at first," Athena related. "Maybe a hundred paces away... among the reeds, over there. It's sort of greyish, and sometimes golden. And I think it's curious about us. *Listening* to us."

Wicklow peered into the darkness beyond the camp. "I see nothing unusual," she said.

"Maybe here in the Scatterlands, the Whisperlights are different," Athena guessed.

"They're still a trap," Wicklow told her.

"There it is!" Athena said, pointing so her friends would see it too. The grey-gold shape hovered over a path, near a broken stone statue of a jackal, a hundred paces away. It had resolved itself some more, so that its wispy outline took on the semblance of arms, hands, and a head; it turned, as though walking, and retreated into the darkness again.

Sylvano and Layla joined them. "Are you seeing that?" Sylvano asked, whispering, pointing at the shape as it floated away down a narrow footpath between the reeds.

Wicklow clamped his hand on Athena's wrist. "Don't follow it," he warned.

"I think it *wants* us to follow it," Athena said.

"Don't," Wicklow repeated.

"I know I've asked a lot of you lately," Athena said. "But I think we have to follow it. Or, *I* have to... and so does Wicklow."

"Was that your plan all along?" Wicklow said. "See, I was under the impression this entire time that *you didn't actually have one* –"

"Of course I have a plan!" Athena protested. Then she softened, as she could read the disbelief on the faces of her friends. "Okay, I don't have a plan," she admitted. "Follow the Whisperlights, Dubhdarra told me. And I did. Somehow the four of us came together, and between us we had everything we needed to make the voyage happen. Layla got us a ship. Wicklow showed us the way to this island. Sylvano's our protector, keeping us safe from the likes of Blackwood and d'Orsonnes, who might have stopped us. We're the *perfect* team for this mission. It's almost as if..."

She paused, and touched the winged rabbit figurine, safe beneath her shift.

"As if someone *arranged* for us to find each other," she finished.

Sylvano said, "Maybe one of the gods is pissed at the others, and he's using us to get back at them."

"Or maybe one of the gods has the same questions we do," said Athena, her face alight with wonder.

The figure beckoning for Athena and her friends to follow was clearer now, though still hazy in his outline. It appeared to be a man of middle years, muscular and tall, with a midnight-blue tunic, and gemstone-studded gold chains about his neck, wrists, waist, and headdress.

Layla leaned to Wicklow and said, "Can the Whisperlights take on human form like that?"

"Maybe *here* they can," the *astron* replied.

Athena rose and took the first few steps toward him. "Layla! Sylvano!

All of you – let's follow him?"

"I'm telling you that isn't wise," said Wicklow.

"Come now," said Athena, "did we sail past the edge of the world just to gather seashells? We were brought here by the gods. Let's find out why!"

And off she went, down a path that had opened among the reeds, following the summoner.

Sylvano shrugged his shoulders. "Might as well go with her," he told the others. "Or else she'll go without us. Again."

They gathered their lamps and their weapons, and explored the path until the light of the campfire was too dim and distant to be seen.

Seeing them go, Etienne tapped two of his sailors on the shoulder. "Follow them," he said.

The men gathered their weapons and crept down the path, like secret hunters in the night.

Cricket songs and nocturnal bird calls surrounded them. A cool breeze carried the scent of dust, cactus flowers, and petrichor. The Whisperlights remained low to the ground, close to the reeds and tallgrasses, until the path came to a stark edge where the riverside wetland ended, and a stone desert began. Stars burned overhead, brighter and clearer than Athena had ever seen them before but the shadowy man carried on. The figure led the four outlaws over the bricks of an ancient road, half-buried under the drifting sand, and half-hidden under the faint light of the two waning moons in the night sky.

Layla turned around to see how far they had gone from camp. When she looked behind her, the desert stretched on to the horizon, with no end.

"How did that happen?" she wondered, worried.

"What?" Athena asked. She too turned around to see the infinite desert behind them, and the road swallowed by sand dunes.

"We're less than a hundred paces from the camp, and we're already lost," Layla said.

As she finished speaking, they found a path ahead flanked by rows of braziers on stone columns. They sparked and flamed to life, and their heir light spread out over the desert. Houses, storefronts, and workshops appeared. Awnings unrolled over windows and rooftops with clay jugs of wine, olive oil, and baskets of spices and grains, were collected beneath the awnings. Small oil lamps lit up on tables and benches along the edges of the street.

Sylvano drew his sword. "I don't like this," he said. "Cities don't just rise up out of nothing."

Wicklow agreed and unsheathed two daggers. "Sorcery," he whispered. "It has to be."

Athena touched a table and slapped her hands on a wall. "Seems solid enough," she reported.

Layla felt even less comfortable. With her wheel-lock pistol ready, she cast her wide eyes down the side alleys and into the open windows. "My grandfather sometimes told us stories of places like this, in the Scatterlands," she said. "Towns that only appeared at night. Cities that seem empty, until you come to the market square. Then, suddenly, everybody jumps out of hiding – and they're werewolves!"

"How did he live to *tell* that kind of tale?" Sylvano asked.

"Some of his men didn't," Layla told him.

Following the widest street, they came to the main town square. A massive temple rose at its far side, its portico flanked by colossal pillars of stone, carved and painted with strange animals, gods in heroic poses, and hieroglyphic writings. Much like Layla's story, they found the square full of people, sitting at long tables, and feasting. A long queue of servants came in and out of the temple, carrying clay jugs of wine and baskets of bread, nuts, and fruit. River-birds and desert creatures lay on one of the tables, ready to be gutted and dressed for the ovens.

The man Athena had persuaded her friends to follow stood near the gate to the temple, directing the servers to the tables. His skin seemed bronze in the moonlight. His beard grew down almost to his navel, braided and bound with gold rings. Noticing the four visitors, he stood up straighter, and approached them, pointing his fingers and calling attention to them: "Outlanders! May all the gods protect us – Outlanders at our festival!"

Everyone dropped their knives and plates and looked to see who the bronze man was pointing to. The musicians stopped in mid-song. Others whispered the word *outlander* among themselves, along with other things in a language Athena felt sure was made for cursing.

Athena grasped the hilt of her sword, in case she needed to draw it.

The bronze man drew near. "I am Auzletun. High priest of the Temple of the Great City of Amen'Ka. Who are you?"

Athena's friends looked to her for initiative.

"I'm Athena Kildare, and... well, we are explorers from Summerland."

"Never since the making of the world has our most holy festival been witnessed by outlanders," Auzletun interrupted to tell her. "And for that, you must pay the price!"

Sylvano nudged Layla. "Flip him a few coins, or something, and then let's get out of here."

"Oh, we do not speak of anything as vulgar as *money* during our festival," Auzletun said to Sylvano. "Your price, for interrupting our sacred rites, is... to take a seat at a table! Come! Eat, drink, all of you, as much as you like. And all praise to the great god Ar'vanor, who brought us new friends to share it with."

The assembly at their tables raised their wine cups and sang out the name of their god in a jubilant invocation: "Ar'vanor! Ar'vanor!"

Athena grinned. She and Sylvano lowered their weapons, but the others kept theirs raised, even as some of the townsfolk approached them and showered handfuls of flower petals over their heads. Sylvano lowered his sword when a shapely and wide-smiling woman offered him a clay goblet of wine. He accepted and thanked her – she kissed him on the cheek.

Layla nudged him in the ribs for it, but then a broad-shouldered and muscular man offered her a similar goblet. She blushed a little and accepted it. Sylvano grinned and nudged her back.

They took a seat at a table near the entrance to the temple. Auzletun sat with them.

"Tell me, please," he said, sitting next to Sylvano. "Where is your country, your Summerland? Is to the west, the east, from here? Is it near, or far?"

"It's to the north-west," Sylvano told him. "Some six weeks of hard sailing away."

"Are there cities like this one? What do you eat there? What are the names of your gods? What songs do you sing for them? What stories do you tell?"

"There are many cities like this one," Sylvano said. "For instance –"

Athena cleared her throat to get attention. "We came here in search of something," she said to Auzletun. "A place called the Gates of the Morning. Do you know it?"

"Oh yes, my friend, we know of the Land of the Dawn, and its many wonders," Auzletun confirmed. "Our historians say that our city was once the crown of a great empire, with a fleet of ships so vast we could conquer whole nations in a single day!"

"And did you have *Navigators* then?" Wicklow asked. "Do you have them still?"

"Navigators?" Auzletun asked, puzzled for the first time.

Wicklow removed his turban, revealing the shape of his ears, the flesh of his head. "People who looked like me, who knew how to find safe paths in sea."

Auzletun studied Wicklow for a moment. Then he made a wide grin and opened his arms. "A pathfinder! Ar'vanor be praised – he has sent us a new pathfinder! The empire of Amen'Ka shall be restored!"

As before, at the mention of the name of their god, the assembly raised their drinking cups and invoked him in a loud chorus: "*Ar'vanor*!"

"No, I'm not," said Wicklow. "I mean... Maybe you have someone here who can teach me?"

"Oh, I beg your forgiveness, I didn't quite hear. You are an *apprentice* pathfinder!" Auzletun said. "All the same, it is a great goodness that Ar'vanor brought you here. Yes, we have a great library, with chronicles, traveller's tales, maps, teachers – everything you need to complete your training. It has been many an age since a ship from Amen'Ka returned to us..." Auzletun's face darkened for a moment. But only a moment and his excitement to share his city with his visitors soon returned. "But come... Tell me more of your Summerland! How did it come by its name? How long is your dry season? When does your rainy season begin? How long are your rivers?"

Layla gave Athena a nudge. "Are we going to answer his questions all night, or can we get some answers out of him, too?"

Athena understood. Turning to Auzletun, she said. "In Summerland, all the kings are tyrants, and all they care about is war. And the merchant-princes are worse – every year they find a new way to turn a profit out of thievery, rape, and murder. I, myself, was stolen from my home when I was only a girl, and all my friends have stories like that of their own. We will answer all your questions and tell you all our stories, if you can help us find the Gates of the Morning."

Auzletun nodded, listening, and thinking. It seemed to Athena that he grasped for the first time that she had a mind of her own.

"We can teach your friend here to be a pathfinder," Auzletun said. "But please... you must understand. You are the first people to come to our land since the last of our ships set out to sea, and never returned. And that was so long ago, there is no one alive who remembers it. You cannot imagine what it is like to live in the unchanging desert. Each day exactly the same as the last. No one to talk to but yourself, for all eternity."

"Eternity?" Athena asked.

Layla said, "How old are you?"

Doubt crossed Auzletun's face. His voice hesitated, searching for the words, but not finding them.

A scuffling sound from across the square distracted him. The two crewmembers sent by Etienne to follow Athena peeked around a corner; one of them dislodged a clay wine-jug from its cradle. It rolled over the cobbles, dispensing its contents on the ground.

"More visitors!" Auzletun exclaimed. He dashed to them and took them by their hands to invite them to the feast. "Father Ar'vanor has blessed us again!"

The assembly raised their wine-cups and hailed the name of their god again: "Ar'vanorrrr!"

"Tell me, please, are you also from Summerland?" Auzletun implored the two sailors. "Or have you come from another great country? Come! Eat, drink, and tell me everything."

Athena looked to her companions. "Etienne must have sent them to follow us," she reasoned.

The two sailors accepted the beer-cups and kisses from the serving-women, grabbing and holding the women much harder and longer than was polite. The women, however, accepted it with grace. Then they sat at the nearest table, while the serving-men placed a platter of bread and roasted fish before them. They took the meat in their hands and bit down with pleasure.

Then they spat the food out. "Sand!" one of them said, disgusted.

Curious, Wicklow took an olive from a nearby bowl and ate it. He, too, spat it out.

"He's right – it's made of sand,", he told his companions.

Sylvano drew his sword at Auzletun. "What are you playing at!" he threatened.

The torches, oil lamps, and brazier-fires all went out, leaving the dim blue grey of the two moons as the only illumination. All around, the serving-women, and the assembly at the tables, faded away into smoke, and the smoke faded into air. The tables, and then the houses around the square, dissolved into sand, falling into heaps on the ground, leaving only a few bare and crumbling stone walls half-buried in the desert. The great temple also fell into sand, leaving some of the ornamental columns standing, but none to the fullness of their original height. Athena and her friends found themselves in the midst of a mere skeleton of a city – cobblestone roads and broken stones, surrounded by the dunes of an endless and relentless desert, and beyond them, the stars of the endless night sky.

Auzletun remained, but his hair and beard thinned, his bones almost visible beneath the parched-dry covering of skin. His gold regalia tarnished, missing its gemstones, and his tunic was threadbare and worn. His face was almost a skull, and his eyes looked without seeing, unblinking, and unmoving.

"What sorcery is this?" Sylvano demanded, pressing his sword on Auzletun's bones.

"Not sorcery... it's necromancy," Wicklow said. "The conjuring of the dead."

Etienne's two sailors were the first to run away, kicking a trail of sand and dust into the air behind them.

"No – please – stay!" Auzletun implored them. "Tell me your stories – don't go!"

But the sailors kept running.

Auzletun made a gesture, reaching out to grasp them and pull them back, even though they were already over a hundred paces away. With his gesture, the sand rose up like a wave, rushed toward the sailors, and swallowed them. They screamed and swept the sand with their swords and fired into it with their pistols. Their weapons gave them no help. The sand grasped them by the legs and the waist and pulled them back to the remains of the old market square, holding them tighter the more they struggled.

"Stay with me," Auzletun pleaded.

But the two sailors were now swallowed by the sand over their heads, their screaming muffled and then silenced.

Auzletun rushed to the dune that took them and spoke to them: "Thank you so much for staying! I'll get you some more wine."

"I don't think he realizes that he just killed them," Athena said, furrowing her brow.

"I think it's time for a strategic retreat," Sylvano suggested.

His friends made no objection. They ran in the direction they thought was toward the ship... down the half-buried remains of the city's main avenue, toward the riverside, and the sea.

"No, please! Don't go!" Auzletun pleaded, his voice anguished. "The silence – the darkness – the burning of the sun! You don't understand!"

He made his gesture again, and the sand rose in answer. It swirled around the four sprinters, chewing at their ankles, whipping their legs. Athena unbuckled her belts and dropped all her weapons so that she might run faster. Seeing her example, the others did the same. Wicklow tripped on a stone, and the sand rose to grasp him by the waist. Sylvano pulled him to his feet again, though this gave the rising sand a grip on his arms. He brushed it off as he ran, though it did not help.

A splash of sand caught Sylvano in the face. He lurched forward to escape it, but inhaled a mouthful of dust, and could not call for help; he made only a gurgling, painful sound that only Layla heard. The sand swallowed his legs and swirled up to his belly.

She grasped his hand. "Hold on!"

But Sylvano could not see her anymore. Desperate to protect his face, his hand slipped out of hers. His eyes closed, he stumbled on, off the trail, and deeper into the desert.

"Sylvano!" Layla shouted.

Hearing this cry of anguish, Athena turned and stopped. The sand rose around her legs and reached her waist. She saw a vague shape that might have been Sylvano, pulling off his coat and fanning the sand and dust away, without effect.

"Take my hand – we'll go together," Athena told Layla. "Wicklow – you too!"

"We can't!' Layla told her. "The sand will take us!"

Somewhere in the distance, faint above the wind, Auzletun's voice continued to cry, "Ar'vanor, don't let them leave me!"

Athena's last glimpse of Sylvano was that of a man with his coat pulled out of his hands by the wind and his hair flying. He had one arm up to protect his face, and the other outstretched to test for obstacles in the path. He staggered away, unaware of where he was going.

He fell into shadow, and from there, into memory.

"Athena – run!" Layla howled.

Layla paused for a heartbeat, seizing the faint hope that she might see

Sylvano again. But the sand rose up to her belly, grasping her wrists, and pulling her back. She ran.

They found the edge of the reeds and palm fronds – a landmark that gave them hope again. The sand receded and the wind faded. They sprinted as fast as possible nonetheless, until they reached the edge of the river. Only then, did they stop to catch their breath and meet each other eye to eye. Their skin was scratched from the stones in the sand, their eyes were sore and red, and their clothes were torn.

And Sylvano was gone.

When her breath returned, Layla marched to Athena, grabbed a handful of pebbles from the shore and threw them at her. "You murderer!" she screeched. "You, stupid, selfish, reckless, little child! Sylvano is dead, and it's your fault!"

With Athena turning her head to protect her face from the stones, Layla reached for her throat.

"That's enough, Layla," said Wicklow, pulling her away. "Sylvano was her oldest friend."

"But he was *my lover*!" Layla howled. She lurched for Athena's throat again, but Wicklow held her back. She collapsed into his arms, then threw him off and staggered a few steps away, to mourn alone.

"It's fine – maybe he's still lost – Dubhdarra can bring him back," Athena said. She reached into her shift to find the token her protector had given her.

But it was lost in the sandstorm. Its empty string dangled from her neck, with a broken wooden loop that once fixed the figurine to its place. She staggered into the reeds, in the direction of the desert, searching around in the dark for Dubhdarra's token, then realizing the gesture was useless.

A banshee wail burst from her breast. She returned to the river and collapsed into it, up to her waist in the water, weeping her loudest, and not caring who could see it or hear it.

When her eyes had no more tears to let fall, and the river drenched her clothes to saturation, she pulled herself back to the shore.

And then, from out of the reeds, from behind the palms, and falling from the stars, came the Whisperlights.

§ 41.

She opened her trembling hands to them. Some of them touched her fingertips and her arms. But for all their wonderful colours, and their different brightnesses, they gave Athena no sense of comfort tonight.

Standing up and turning around, she expected to see the same shade who had appeared to her when she entered the Whisperlights back before the voyage began. Instead, standing perhaps a hundred paces away, she saw what looked like her childhood home in the village of Cherry Grove: its heavy logs for the ground floor walls, its high-pitched roof with the window gables and the red clay tiles. The door was open and a warm glow came from inside, telling her the fireplace was lit.

"Auzletun!" she shouted. "If that's just another of your sandcastles, then I'm not going anywhere near it."

She reached to her waist to grasp her sword, then she remembered she had cast it off while running out of the desert. She looked around for anything else she could use as a weapon – a stick, a rock... Nothing.

A familiar voice spoke from somewhere in the darkness: "Athena! Come inside and close the door! Bandits everywhere, these days."

"Father?" Athena asked, recognizing his voice.

"Inside, inside!" Father's voice urged her.

Cautious, but also curious, she stepped inside. The fire blazed warm and welcoming in the fireplace. Father's favourite wicker chair stood near it, and on it sat a basket covered in a kitchen cloth. It contained a dozen honey-rolls, a favourite taste from her childhood. Everything about the house was as she remembered it from the last day before the army burned it down. The smells of charcoal and wood smoke, the sight of the whitewash on the clay walls and the red ochre on the door frames, and the sounds of the wooden window shutters knocking in the breeze along with the creak of the floorboards beneath her feet. The one new presence in the room was the cloud of Whisperlights, exploring alongside and around her.

"We are so glad you came home again," said Mother, her voice coming from another room. "You look like you're carrying the weight of the world. What happened?"

"Sylvano died today," Athena informed her. She moved to the kitchen, looking for Father. There she found everything in its usual place: cooking pots, wooden mixing spoons, bowls, knives, and jars. But still no sign of Father.

"We were caught in a sandstorm, trying to escape from… it's hard to describe," Athena said.

"Sylvano? The boy whose mother is a *strega*?" said Mother, again sounding from the next room.

"Yes, him – where are you?" Athena called out. "Easier to talk to you when I can see you."

"We're just over here," Mother said.

Athena followed the sound of her voice to the narrow ladder-steps that led to the attic. Climbing it, she found the two stools by the window, and the cloth that Mother had used to bring her the honey-rolls, where she left them on the night of the storm. Whisperlights glowed in the half-darkness. Neither Father nor Mother were there.

"Still can't find you," Athena said.

"So, was it bandits who got him?" said Father. This time, his voice seemed to come from everywhere and nowhere, above and below.

Athena tried to open the window, and found it was locked. It was a surprising discovery, as she didn't know it was possible to lock them from inside. "No, it was some kind of necromancer in the desert…"

Before she could relate more of the story, the emptiness rose in her belly, and the strength drained out of her limbs.

"And it wouldn't have happened," Athena said, her frustration with the window growing, "if not for me."

"If not for you?" Mother asked.

"It was my fault," Athena said. "I was so certain we were on the right path. I thought, sure it's dangerous, but it'll be all right. Dubhdarra put us together. He made us the perfect team – we can do anything!"

"So, you opened the door without thinking, again," Father said. "Just like on the night of the storm. And this time, the stranger was a bandit. Didn't I tell you everyone has to be a bandit these days, to survive?"

Athena nodded, acquiescing. "My life was supposed to be different," she sighed. "I was going to walk my dog in the hills and pick wild cherries off the trees. Maybe fall in love. And just do... I don't know – whatever it is normal people do."

She climbed down the stairs, looking for him. She peeked into her parents' bedroom. The wardrobe was open, but empty; as she recalled, her parents owned only two suits of clothing anyway. Most of it hung from hooks or lay in a crumpled pile in the wardrobe. The blankets on the bed were in disarray and a pair of her mother's shoes lay on their sides, near the door. The basket where Buddy the dog normally slept still held his woollen blanket, and was still covered in his rough hair, but no living thing slept there.

"Why do we have to talk like this – with you always in the next room?" Athena asked.

Father's voice ignored the question. "I made some fresh bread for you. It's on the kitchen table. And your mother made honey-rolls and jam."

Athena looked into the kitchen and found the food in a cloth-lined basket. She nibbled on a honey-roll, careful in case it was sand, but found it was honey-roll.

"Nice," she said.

"It's always been your favourite," said Mother. "Your bedsheets are freshly washed, and there's new straw in the mattress. Your father and I are glad you came home."

Father said, "Take a seat by the fire. Sit in *my* chair, if you want – the big one, with the cushion. It's time to rest now. Lay your troubles down."

In the front room, Athena found the fire warm and welcoming. There was a comfortable chair with cushions and blankets, a stool for her feet, and a cup of warm tea at a side-table. She tasted the tea – it was fruity and flavourful, and made her smile. She sat in Father's chair and enjoyed the food and the warmth for a moment.

Soon, however, she felt a need to ask, "Is this real?"

"Of course, Athena," said Father. "It's everything that was taken away from us. We worked so hard to get it back."

"Then why is it the same as it was before?" Athena asked. "And I mean, *exactly* the same. As if the last seven years didn't happen."

"Dear child, it's been only two months," Mother said.

Athena's heartbeat quickened. Her breath held in her throat for a moment.

Mother's voice continued, "And now you can have the *life* that was taken from you. You'll grow up as you should have. You could learn the cooper's trade, like Father did, if you like. Or follow my old trade, weaving a loom? Humble professions, but honest ones."

The idea was tempting. Her fingers ran across the blanket that draped over the back of Father's chair.

Father's voice crooned on, "You have to ask yourself... what do you really *want* in life? Where do you want to go? Who do you want to be?"

Fair questions, Athena thought, even if there was something insidious hidden behind their utterance.

"I want to be who I am *now,*" Athena said.

"But you are the woman whose childish bravado got your best friend killed!" Father reminded her, a note of sternness returning to his voice.

And it was true, Athena knew. That was the problem. She slumped into Father's chair and stared into the fire.

"There, that's better, isn't it?" Mother's voice soothed her. "Take a rest, for a while. Think things over. There are as many paths before you as there are birds in the sky. Which way will you fly, young Athena? Perhaps you'd like to find a boy you could love and have a family of your own with him. Plenty of eligible young men in the villages around here. Just think of it... sitting by your own fire in your own cottage, surrounded by loving children. Drinking warm tea on cold nights. Proud of yourself for putting in a full day of good hard work."

Athena *could* think of it, and the thought warmed her belly. It was satisfying and peaceful. She sat with the feeling, and let it spread to her fingers and toes.

Then she asked, "Would that be all? Would there be nothing more?"

"Why would you want anything more?" Father asked her. "You'd have everything you need for a long and peaceful life. Friends, family, a home, good food –"

"What about *answer_*?" Athena said, perking her head up.

"You would have none of the disturbances in life that lead to hard *questions*," Father's voice promised.

"So, in other words, *no*... right?" Athena said. "No answers?"

Mother said, "No sadness, no struggle, no impossible odds, no broken hearts, no unfulfilled dreams –"

"No storms over the hills – is that what you're saying?" Athena replied. "No ships that fly to the Scatterlands? Sea turtles the size of islands? What about curiosity? What about passion? What about..." she struggled to find the words, " what about cracking open the shell of the world, to see what's really inside? And if it turns out the world is rotten through and through, what about doing something about it? Summerland was supposed to be beautiful!"

"No death," Father said, plain and powerful.

Athena paused, and said, "But no one can promise that. Sylvano might have died some other way. Or it might have been *me*, lost in the desert. Death comes for *everyone* eventually, doesn't it? And when he comes for me, I want to have a good story to tell him. Of course, I'm gutted that Sylvano is gone – how could I not be? But I don't want his death to be for nothing. And I want *my* life to be about *something*."

Mother and Father did not speak, though their presence remained palpable, and near. Athena waited for a reply as the fire burned lower, and the sand gritted on the windows in the wind.

Soon she decided she had waited long enough. She rose and moved to the cottage door. "I'm going back to my ship," she said. "And I'm going to find the Gates of the Morning. I'm doing this for you, too."

Athena pulled herself to her feet and took a long last look at the image of her childhood home as it faded back into the night.

"Remember us, Athena," said the voice of her mother.

"I will," she promised.

She closed the door. And the desert was silent again.

§ 42.

Athena followed her footsteps in the sand back to the marsh, and to the river. There she found Dubhdarra, surrounded by Whisperlights, sitting on a tree-stump and feeding some fish in the river. His winged rabbit sat on the ground nearby. He smiled upon seeing her and opened his hands to great her.

She ran to him and hugged him. They then sat on the shore together. Dubhdarra unrolled a honey-roll from a cloth and offered it to her.

"Your fetch came to see me, when he fell off that string around your neck," Dubhdarra explained. "He told me what happened to Sylvano."

"I lost him in the desert," Athena mourned. "It's all my fault!"

Dubhdarra gave her a warm consoling hug.

"You were right about the Whisperlights, you know," Dubhdarra told her, when he let her go. "They're teachers, of a sort. Have you noticed the kind of situations in which they appear?"

Athena thought about it. "Whenever something bad happens?" she asked.

"It also helps if you're close to a swamp, or river, or a really thick forest," Dubhdarra added. "Here's another secret about Summerland – she's a living thing in her own right. She has feelings, like you, and the Whisperlights are her healing organ."

"The Whisperlights... they're healing me?" Athena wondered.

"They're helping you heal yourself," Dubhdarra said. "But only because you were straight with them about what happened, and what you want out of life. I'm sorry it took Sylvano's death to teach you the difference between courage and recklessness. But you can honour him by taking that lesson to heart and picking your battles from now on with more care."

"Can you bring him back?" Athena asked, pleading.

Dubhdarra shook his head. "No... I'm sorry."

Athena looked down. "I didn't think so. But I had to ask."

Dubhdarra made a compassionate smile. He rose and invited Athena to rise with him. "I believe it's time for you to decide whether to go on with this quest of yours, or whether to take your friends home while you still can."

"Where are they?" Athena asked.

§ 43.

On the slope of a sand dune, Layla beheld her family's palazzo, dappled with the colours of the Whisperlights, its front doors opened and inviting her within. Uncle Crave emerged, in the front seat of a horse-drawn carriage. He was dressed in mourner's black from his boots to his hat. His expression, however, showed no grief or remorse. Instead it was something like the satisfaction of knowing a dangerous secret. He looked down to Layla and offered his hand to lift her up to sit beside him.

"You were always my favourite, Layla," he said. "Come, it's time you joined the family business."

Wicklow found himself at the edge of the river, facing a cloud of Whisperlights a short distance upstream. He held his muscles, and his breath, at their sight. The cloud neither approached him nor receded away. It simply remained, inviting him and waiting, as it had once done for his father, and so many others before. The *astron* regarded it for a long moment, at first through the side of his eye, while his belly rebelled within him. Everything he thought he knew about the Whisperlights rushed through his mind.

Among those recollections, another necessity called to him, and it warmed his long-hidden courage.

He unravelled his turban and dropped it to the ground and walked toward them.

§ 44.

"They're only a short way behind you," Dubhdarra answered Athena, reassuring her. "They shall have things to tell you, when you see them."

Athena turned to face the riverside, to rejoin her friends. "Are you ever going to tell me who you are... who you *really* are?" she asked.

"I believe I *have*, several times," Dubhdarra grinned. He took some food from a pouch on his belt and fed it to an ibis that landed nearby.

"But I saw you fall from the sky, like a flock of birds," Athena insisted. "How is it you could do that? Did you come from... from *above*?"

Dubhdarra's expression grew amazed. "You *saw* that? Very few ever do!"

"I *have* to know," she said.

The old ranger nodded. "First of all, my name really is Dubhdarra Muirthemney," he assured her. "And I'm a kind of messenger. The gods sometimes need someone to make the rounds, in Summerland. Tend the flowers... see the small picture. Find people who can realize the beauty that the gods intended for this world and bring them together."

Athena's mouth dropped with awe as Dubhdarra spoke. Her eyes widened; her fingers trembled. When she recovered herself, she remembered that her three calls for his help were now all spent.

"Will I ever see you again?" she asked.

Dubhdarra said, "I don't know."

Athena stepped up and hugged him again. Dubhdarra kissed her on the forehead.

She wanted to stay in his company, ask him more questions, and hear his stories. However, Athena knew their time together was complete. Any further lingering would spoil it, like fine wine left to become vinegar. Most people are lucky to have one encounter with a messenger from gods; Athena had four of them. From now on, what luck remained in her life, she would have to create for herself.

She waved goodbye, careful not to say the word, lest it became the last thing she ever said to him. Dubhdarra waved long and slow for her, in return; he pressed his palms together, touching his fingertips to his lips, to bless her for the journey.

Then Athena ambled her way along the riverside to rejoin her friends.

§ 45.

She found Layla sitting up to her waist in the water. Some of her clothes were torn. Her face was tired, and her eyes red and long from hours of unrelenting weeping.

"Should have known this would happen," said Layla, when she noticed Athena sitting down beside her. "It's all your fault, you know."

"Yes, it is," Athena said.

Layla did not expect that response.

"You were right about me," Athena continued. "I *was* stupid and reckless. And because of that, I got my oldest friend killed."

"You didn't know him like I did," Layla chided her.

"That's true," Athena agreed. "I'm not trying to say my pain is worse than yours. I'm trying to apologize."

Layla faced Athena, her eyes narrowed, her mouth tensed. "You think you can make everything better with an apology?" she snapped. "You don't know what I lost when I lost him! He was going to be my escape from House Darvi, and all its stupid obsessions. We were going to run away, change our names, and start a new life. And you, you feckless country clodhopper – you were supposed to save the world!"

Athena looked to the ground.

Then Layla softened. "I was going to order the ship to turn around and go home," she said. "I was going to leave you marooned here. But the Whisperlights showed me what would happen if I did that. I'd put myself on a path toward becoming exactly like my family. I know it was that creature in the desert who killed Sylvano, not you. But it's going to be a while before I can look at you, and not see *him*."

Athena nodded and thought it best to say nothing.

"Now, let's find the others," Layla suggested.

They followed the riverside together, walking side by side, neither speaking nor looking at each other.

They found Wicklow seated beneath a tree in a cross-legged posture, his hands folded in his lap, his eyes closed, and his face peaceful. A few of the whispers still surrounded him.

"Wicklow?" Athena asked, uncertain whether it was safe to approach him.

Wicklow's eyes opened. They glowed a soft shade of cyan now. He smiled for them.

"Are you okay?" Layla asked him.

"I'm fine," he said. "The lights have shown me many things. Each of us are smaller than grains of dust in the ocean, compared to all of Summerland; and Summerland itself is a grain of dust compared to all the stars."

"Sounds... depressing," said Athena.

"It is nothing of the sort," said Wicklow, rising to his feet. "It is, in fact, quite magnificent. For I have a mind; I can *conceive* this immensity, grasp it, reason about it, *witness* it. Such was the test the Whisperlights gave me, and for my reward, I am a Navigator."

§ 46.

At the camp on the beach, the crew had gathered around a fire to cook their freshly caught fish and seabirds. Etienne paced around the perimeter. Seeing Athena approach, he struck a judgmental pose.

"Perhaps you thought it terribly *funny* to wander off without escort into a city full of ghosts, without telling your ship's first mate, or taking your captain and your Navigator with you!" he said. Then, taking a second look, "Where's your marksman? What's his name – Sylvano?"

"The desert took him," Athena said.

"He knew the risks going in, as do we all," said Etienne, without hesitation or remorse – a plain fact of life, long accepted. To Layla he said, "Any last orders for tonight, captain?" The way he accented the words *last orders* made Layla shudder.

"Let the crew rest and enjoy themselves," Layla said. "Tomorrow morning, we fly for Dawnland."

"And, you know the way?" Etienne asked.

Wicklow said, "Yes, I do."

Etienne noted the change in the glow of Wicklow's eyes. "Our first profitable discovery of the voyage," he said.

While her friends sat by the fire to take some food, Athena wandered a short distance away. It was not quite out of range of the firelight, but far enough to be alone. She removed the string that once held Dubhdarra's winged rabbit and contemplated it for a while.

She built a small cairn from nearby stones and left the string around it.

§ 47.

The snappers crawled up from the sea in the morning and nibbled at the sailor's toes. Startled into full wakefulness, the crew scooped them up with shovels and threw them back into the sea.

Returning to the *Sun Dog*, Athena sat in the stern of the shore-boat, absorbing the sight of the last place where she saw Sylvano alive. Layla sat with her for the same reason. They did not speak to each other, but when they reached the ship, they shared a knowing, accepting glance. Athena considered that a small victory.

Wicklow took the Navigator's traditional position, seated on a small platform near the ship's wheel. He held the map in his hands but closed his eyes.

"It's not fair, you know," said Etienne, looking at Wicklow.

"What's not fair?" Athena asked.

"That only *they* can do it!"

Athena didn't like how Etienne pronounced the word *they*. She smiled awkwardly. "Maybe you can ask the gods why they wanted it that way."

Etienne shook his head. "Ask yourself this," he said. "What if *anyone* can learn it, but the fucking fringers keep the secret to themselves? So that we don't round them all up and throw them back into whatever abyss they came from?"

He laughed, and some of the crew nearby laughed with him.

But Athena glared at him. "What if he refuses to take us anywhere because he heard you say that?"

Etienne gave her a look of disgust. "If he doesn't take us where we tell him to, what if we killed him?" he asked. It was not a question.

The nearby crewmates laughed again, enjoying the idea.

"And then, where would you find another Navigator?" Athena asked.

Etienne dismissed her question with a wave. "Anywhere," he said.

Athena wanted to reply, but Wicklow's shouting took her attention. "Ship ahoy!"

Layla took up her spyglass to see where Wicklow was pointing. She spotted another schooner, all sails flying, and her side-sails unfolding.

"Looks like the same ship that followed us out of port," said Layla. "How did they find us?"

"Easy enough to find a ship, as it is to find an island, when you have a Navigator," said Etienne, smirking.

"Deploy side-sails," Layla ordered.

"No clouds to hide in, this time," Etienne reminded her.

"Set the sails anyway," Layla said. "At least we can keep them from catching up to us."

Etienne shrugged and delivered the orders to the crew.

§ 48.

The *Sun Dog* sailed into stranger, darker seas.

Near nightfall, the watch spotted a long serpentine creature, whose head was wreathed with antlers, slithering in the water. It reached up to snap its jaws at the ship, but a quick action from the pilot ensured it could not reach high enough. Another day, they passed a family of stone-fleshed giants walking in the sea, tall enough that the surface of the water came only to their elbows. A white froth swirled behind them on the surface of the sea.

The ship following them was always within sight – a lingering thorn in Athena's uneasy mind.

"We are only two more nights away from our destination," Wicklow announced.

But with the rising of the sun so close, a great wind also rose, pushing back on the *Sun Dog* and throwing her off course.

"What's wrong with the dynamo?" Layla asked, her voice urgent and panicked.

"Nothing," said Etienne. "It's just not strong enough to counter this wind."

The crew strained and heaved on the ropes to keep the ship level and airborne, lest it tip all its people overboard, or crash into the water. Despite their best efforts, some of the ropes slipped out of sweaty hands and whipped over the deck, slashing one crewmate in the face.

"We have to take in the sails," Etienne told Layla, shouting over the wind.

"We can't," Layla said. "That other ship will catch up to us!"

"They're caught in the same wind we are," Etienne told her.

Layla saw the sense in it and nodded. "Take in the sails," she acquiesced.

Etienne gave the orders, and reduced the fore and aft sails to half-mast. The crew was glad to oblige, though the job was no less easy. Etienne himself climbed the foremast to release the sail from its uppermost catch. Then he slid down one of the ropes and landed on the deck, to a hero's welcome from the crew.

"Tack into the wind, until we can push forward again," he ordered, and the crew jumped to obey.

Athena pursed her lips. In the spyglass, she saw that the pursuing ship had also taken in their side-sails, but they were still following.

"I think they got closer," she said.

§ 49.

"Land ho!" shouted Athena, when she saw the rising, rolling outline of a rocky coastline ahead, in the fading orange red of evening that day.

Wicklow moved to the bow to get a closer look for himself. The glow of his eyes brightened when he saw it. "Dawnland," he declared.

"And the Gates of the Morning? Are they close?" Athena asked him.

"Not far, as the wren flies," Wicklow reported. "One more day."

Layla understood. "Athena, take the wheel. Find somewhere in this landscape where we can shelter for the night, and then set her down. The morning wind is sure to be worse here."

"Aye, captain, aye," Athena said, and she took the wheel.

They sailed on, dipping lower to the ground to get a better view of the landscape, under the silver light of the two moons. The landscape was a corduroy of hills and valleys, steep, rough, and jagged; the hills often crowned with sharp rocky towers like knives. No trees or shrubbery gave a mantle to the land and only thick and spiky grasses gave the stony landscape flesh. On the towers, only mosses grew. Athena surmised that these were the only forms of life that would long survive the daily blasting of the wind from the rising morning sun. Indeed, she soon noticed that the hills were more like carvings in the land, as they all lined up in the direction Wicklow guided them – carvings blasted there by hundreds of sunrises every year for billions of years.

"Was all the world like this, at the beginning?" Athena wondered aloud.

"There's a lake!" Layla said, pointing to a dark patch in the landscape below.

Athena guided in the ship closer. The lake lay in the lee of a low cliff where it seemed the ship could be safe from the morning wind. Along its banks, a flock of gazelles gathered. They were sipping at the water's edge and rubbing each other's necks; sheltering from the morning, just like ourselves, Athena thought. Though the moonlight was dim and silvery, their coats rippled and glowed with gold, creating little pools of light around each of them, mesmerizing all who saw them. As the ship descended, Athena saw the glint of bronze on their antlers. She realized she had seen one of these magnificent creatures before – stuffed and mounted as a display in the Darvi family palazzo.

"Any one of those animals is worth a king's ransom," Etienne said, making casual conversation with Layla, who held the spyglass. "And here's a whole *flock* of them. Name any city in Summerland... with the pelts from those things, you could *buy* it!"

Layla knew that the voyage had to pay for itself somehow, but something in Etienne's tone reminded her that he could not be trusted.

"Any sign of our escort?" Etienne asked.

"None... thank the gods," Layla reported, searching the sky for Blackwood's ship. "I think we lost them."

Etienne grinned. "Right! Gentlemen!" he addressed the crew. "I'd say we've found something that makes this ridiculous and painful charade of an expedition *worth* the long and sorry while. Wouldn't you agree?"

The crew agreed, with enthusiasm.

Etienne marched to the wheel and said to Athena, "Take the ship down to the lake."

Athena did not move. "I take my orders from the captain, not from you," she reminded him.

The crew laughed among themselves. Etienne chuckled with them. Then he drew his pistol and aimed for Athena's head. "Take the ship down," he ordered.

Athena's impulse was to draw her own sword against Etienne, somehow to disarm him, then engage the rest of the crew in a daring tumult of swordplay and bravado. Athena also knew that would be mistaking recklessness for courage again. Courage, in this instance, called for her to choose her moment.

And this wasn't it. Not yet.

"All right," she said. "Taking her down. No one has to get hurt."

Etienne grinned, enjoying his victory as much as he enjoyed the thought of getting rich. He holstered his pistol and issued his orders to the crew. "Take in the sails! Douse the dynamo! Prepare to drop anchor! And take an extra dram of rum – when we get home, we're going to be rich!"

Layla and Wicklow gave Athena puzzled looks.

The crew, cheering for Etienne, ran to their tasks with enthusiasm. The ship splashed down on the lake and dropped anchor. The crew loaded the boats with guns, powder kegs, and butcher knives, then raced to the shore, eager to begin what they called "the hunt." The gazelles seemed puzzled and even curious about these new arrivals at their lake. Their big and innocent eyes regarded the hunters without flinching. Some even took a few brave steps closer. The crew walked up to their prey, touched them, laughed about the ease of the capture.

Etienne took the one standing nearest to him by the antlers, and slashed its throat from ear to ear, felling him on the spot.

Seeing the example, the rest of the crew did the same. When the gazelles saw their brethren falling, they ran. But the crew was ready for this and opened fire with pistols and muskets, felling more. Within mere minutes, almost half the herd were carcasses on the ground. The surviving animals dashed about the field and the slopes of the cliff, panicked and frenzied, looking for an escape. Unfortunately, the glow of their pelts in the pre-dawn light gave them away and they made easy targets for the lazy marksmen.

Athena witnessing the spectacle from the deck of the ship and chose another word for the occasion. "This isn't a hunt; it's a *slaughter*," she said.

When every gazelle in the herd was either dead or had escaped, the crew dropped their weapons and celebrated the money they were sure each pelt would return for them. They hugged each other and began the careful process of field-dressing the animals to take the pelts off the carcasses. They loaded the first batch of pelts on to the *Sun Dog*.

The scene came to a sudden end when an explosion sounded from across the far side of the lake, echoing among the rocky peaks that surrounded the lake and its valley. A moment later, a patch of the ground in the centre of the killing field erupted into a crater, scattering soil, rock and two stag carcasses all around. Everyone turned to find the source of the disruption.

Blackwood's ship swung around from behind a rock peak. Its cannons fired another shot. The deafening din echoed from everywhere again. A spray of buckshot pellets struck the ground close to the water's edge, sending panicked crewmen running left and right.

Etienne, though caught off guard like the rest, collected his wits. "Don't stand in groups!" he ordered the men. "Don't give them a target. Spread out! Make them come to ground. Reload your weapons and prepare for battle!"

A cannonball from Dane's ship struck near the crest of the cliff that protected the lake from the sunrise. Stone shrapnel showered on the men below. They scattered away, covering their heads with their arms.

Athena and Wicklow ran for the protection of the lower deck, but Layla lingered, exposed.

"They're not firing on us; we're actually safe here," she observed.

"That only means they're here for our bounties," Athena said.

"How do you know?" Wicklow asked.

"Is there anything *else* on board that they might want?" Athena said.

"Those stag pelts, maybe," Layla said.

"But they couldn't have known about them before getting here," Athena said, lost in thought for a moment. Then she waved at Blackwood's ship and jumped up and down.

"Dane! Help us, save us!" she shouted.

"What the hell are you doing!" Layla seethed at her.

"Roll with this – it'll work," Athena replied. Then she shouted at Blackwood's ship again, "Please, save us! They kidnapped us – they're going to kill us!"

Dane's ship changed its angle of flight and descended.

"They're going to board us," Wicklow exclaimed.

"That's the idea," Athena told him, smiling.

Etienne, on the ground, reached the same conclusion. He rallied his men back to the shore boats. "Quick, men! Back to the ship – don't let them take the ship!"

Athena grinned. She moved to the helm, where she could see Dane's men on one side, preparing to rappel down to the *Sun Dog* on ropes, and d'Orsonnes' crew racing across the lake on their shore-boats, each side desperate to reach the ship first.

Dane Blackwood touched her boots on the deck at the same moment Etienne d'Orsonnes swung his legs over the railing. Both dashed across the deck, meeting their swords to each other's hearts at the same moment, almost on the centreline of the ship.

"Blackwood," Etienne greeted her in a terse tone.

"D'Orsonnes," Dane returned the greeting. "I see why you left Port Vivaldi in such a hurry. Can't have the whole world knowing where your employer's wealth comes from. Only now, *we* know where it comes from. So, we'll be taking a share for ourselves."

Athena's eyes widened. Dane was not here for the ransom money she might get for deserters. She was here for a much more valuable payoff. The source of the Darvi family wealth was not the pelts of the Dawnland gazelles. It was the knowledge of the location of their grazing grounds.

And Athena had stolen it.

"Wicklow – give me the map," she whispered to her friend.

Behind their backs, so neither Dane nor Etienne could see, Wicklow passed it to her.

"You're a woman of high ambitions, and I admire you for it," Etienne said to Dane, in a tone that was anything but admiring. "But you'll be going home empty-handed, all the same. What would our good employer say if I let you pilfer his treasury?"

"You're the one doing the pilfering here, you turncoat!" Dane told him, her anger rising. "You fled at full sail out of the city, and half an hour later the master noticed one of his maps was missing. I'd say it's an open question whether he knows you're here at all!"

"What map?" Etienne asked.

Layla sensed an opportunity. "It's true," she said, stepping forward. "At the masquerade ball in my uncle's palazzo, Monsieur d'Orsonnes seduced me, and promised to marry me, if I showed him the family secret vault. I took him down there – foolish of me, I admit – and he stole the map, and then held me prisoner on this ship!"

Dane smirked at her. "Etienne here has always wanted a seat at a gentleman's table. He'll do anything to get it."

Etienne d'Orsonnes' jaw dropped. "I would no more seduce this pampered, self-absorbed little child, than I would the master's own mother!"

"But I'm right about what you want," Dane snapped back. She flashed her sword up, threatening Etienne in the face. "And what I want is the map," she demanded. "Now."

Desperation grew in Etienne's voice. "It must have been *her* who stole it," he said, pointing at Athena. "You and I chased her across the city, remember?"

Dane's attention turned to Athena, as did every sailor who had climbed on board the *Sun Dog* from both crews. Athena held up the map for all to see; and she shrugged, as though it were a mere bauble, and stealing it was a lark.

"Athena Kildare," Dane said, recognizing her. "There's a bounty on your head. I'll be taking that, too."

"And you can have her," Etienne said, his confidence returned, "for a price."

The tallgrasses on the crest of the cliff top stirred. Then ripples formed on the surface of the lake. Athena decided this was her moment.

"But isn't this map worth more than the treasure it leads to?" Athena asked. "With this, you can always come back for more."

She gestured to the shore, where more than two dozen Dawnland gazelle pelts still waited to be transported to the ship. Some of them still glowed a faint tawny gold under the brightening pre-dawn sky.

Dane looked. Her eyes widened. Ignoring the threatening sword-points raised by Etienne's crew, she wandered across the deck for a better view.

"He told me there were only ten of those things in the whole world," Dane said, her gaze transfixed.

Etienne stepped in front of her. "They're mine," he grunted. "We found them first. We caught them. We skinned them. They're mine! But we'll give you a cut, if you keep this unfortunate misunderstanding between ourselves," he offered.

Dane surveyed the deck and calculated her odds. "Or I could kill you, and take them all," she said.

Etienne immediately lunged with his rapier. Dane parried it with ease. The move was the spark that ignited both crews to reach for their weapons and fight.

Athena stepped back, folded her arms, and grinned.

Wicklow said to her, "How did you know?"

Athena shrugged. "Didn't you tell me yourself – their only loyalty is to money."

The gentle flittering of the wind gathered strength. Athena had to grab her hat before it was thrown off her head.

"Let's get below deck, shall we?" Athena suggested to her friends.

They crept to the hatch nearest them, trusting that the sailors were too busy fighting each other to notice. They locked the hatch behind them, then ran through the ship to the second hatch to lock it down as well.

A front of hot air rushed over the cliff and eddied around the hollow in the hills that held the lake. Pebbles and small rocks blew over the clifftop and pummelled the lake. Athena trusted that if the lake had survived here for this long, she and the ship would survive here too. However, it might not be safe for the two crews of sailors busy fighting each other to notice the change in the weather. She heard the sounds of the men on the deck shouting and yelping as the stones struck them. There were also the distinct splashes of men thrown off the deck by the wind and their cries for help. There were also the guttural groans of men killed by others, while they scrambled for shelter. The popping of pistols and muskets, the fists banging on the hatches and demands that they should be opened… the threatening… the pleading. And then… silence.

When the time felt right, Athena started a fire in the ship's dynamo.

Outside, the first rays of the sun breached the crest of the cliff, bringing with it a light and gentle warmth. The two crews, having been blown off the deck of the ship, and into the lake were too wounded to fight... but they were alive. Etienne and Dane had taken shelter behind some boulders on the shore, and most of the others had found shelter in the lee of Blackwood's ship, which lay on the far shore of the lake. Its sails were punctured with hundreds of holes.

Meanwhile, the *Sun Dog* rose above the water, where no one could climb back on board. Athena and her friends returned to the deck and stood looking down over Dane and Etienne, guns at the ready, owning their moment.

"Here's what's going to happen," Athena told them. "The both of you, and both crews, will get on Dane's ship. You'll sail for home and you'll leave the *Sun Dog* to the three of us."

"Don't be stupid, Athena," said Dane. "You can't sail a schooner with only three crew!"

"That will be *our* problem, not yours," Athena said.

"We'll hunt you down to the last island for this!" Etienne threatened.

"Why bother?" Layla shouted back to him. "You're going to be rich!"

Etienne and Dane despaired at the sight of the gazelle pelts flying away on the last dregs of the morning wind, tarnished and ruined by the battering of stones. Layla grinned.

The *Sun Dog* lifted over the ridge and into the open sky. Wicklow gave them a bearing, and Athena guided the wheel. They waved good-bye to the men on the lake, who shouted obscenities and fired muskets – all to no effect.

Once they were out of sight of the lake, Athena sat down on the deck near the bow, facing the east. She took off her hat, loosened her weapon-belts, and closed her eyes.

Layla asked her, "Are you injured?"

"No," said Athena. "It just occurred to me... this is the first moment since I was taken from my home that I don't have to be what other people want me to be."

Layla opened her arms, inviting Athena to hold her for a while.

Athena accepted.

§ 50.

They waited until after the following morning's wind before setting sail again. Wicklow and Layla struggled with the forward sail while Athena handled the helm. In weeks of the voyage, they had gained some experience with sail-rigging, but they were still green, and they knew it. They did the best they could.

The hulks and skeletons of old ruined ships lay all over the land before them. They consisted of everything from previous explorers and adventurers, to religious seekers and treasure hunters. The three Summerlanders wondered about each of them in their hearts, lest they meet the same fate.

One night on their voyage, the crew saw that the stars changed colour, and the Night Road brightened. The northern auroras danced among them, sometimes dipping low enough to set the ship's masts alight with green and purple auras of their own.

As the soft glow of pre-dawn appeared in the east, the silhouette of two magnificent obelisks appeared before them, almost tall enough to scratch the clouds. Beyond them, a mile-high cliff overlooked the sea.

"The Gates of Morning," Wicklow declared.

Doing their best to land the ship with care, they skidded across a field of stones, lichens, and heather. The ship lurched to a stop when it hit an outcropping of bedrock. It settled on its side, throwing everything on board against the wall, and much of what was on the top deck spilled overboard.

"I think she'll never berth on the water again," Layla said. "My uncle will never forgive me."

"Sure he will, when he sees what we're bringing back," Wicklow reminded her.

"As long as this ship can take us home," Athena replied.

They followed a rough path suggested by the contours of the land. The dawn chorus of birds began when the east horizon flushed with the first violet and cyan of the morning. By this point, the party had made most of their way to the obelisks. A low stone platform lay before the space between the two massive stones, which now towered over them. As Athena set her foot upon it, a crack of thunder rolled out of the east and across the sky. Clouds formed, dissipated, and formed again, in the speed of a breath. Between them, the stars hid their faces behind the growing colours of sunrise – purple, red, and orange. A flame kindled in the sky, shining upon the obelisks, the clouds, the land, and the three seekers before the immensity.

"Maybe we're not supposed to step on that," Wicklow suggested.

"We came this far," Athena said.

A light flashed on the horizon, bright and clear as the truth, heralded by another crack of thunder. It grew into the limb of the sun, and its wreath of white fire generated the first blast of the morning wind, whipping Athena's hair. As the faces of the three seekers lit up with its blessing, a voice spoke to them from across the sea, rumbling the rocks and blowing the clouds away:

Who approaches the Gates of Morning?

Athena looked to her friends, almost dumb struck with surprise that the old legend about the Gates was true.

"Go on, talk to them," Layla urged her.

Athena felt she had to shout to make her reply heard. "I am Athena Kildare," she called to the sun. "These are my friends... Layla and Wicklow. We have questions!"

Ask, and we shall answer, the voice invited, rumbling the rocks again, and causing one of the ancient shipwrecks behind her to collapse.

Athena collected herself and searched her heart for the words. She found all the anger, despair, and pain that she had been keeping to herself for seven years. They rose up within her, from her toes to her crown, and erupted in a torrent of fury.

"Where are you when we need you!" she raged. "Where were you when my family was stolen from our home? When they burned my village? When they took half the world prisoner and killed half the rest? Where were you when they crushed the Movement in Port Vivaldi – when good people lost, and the spiral of tyrants carried on? Why do our leaders always turn into monsters? And why don't you do anything about it? What were you doing when Sylvano died – why did you let that happen! He was a wounded and angry man trying to become a better man! He gave up revenge, he fell in love, and did everything you told us a good man is supposed to do. He died anyway. Don't you care about us? Didn't you want this world to be beautiful? What's beautiful about children dying of hunger, when there's plenty of food around? What's beautiful about people who can't find a home, because the landlords want more money? What's beautiful about plagues? Or hatred? Or greed? Where are you when we're lonely? Or when we're afraid? Where are you when we call out to you in the middle of the night, and nobody answers back? Are you not listening? Can you not hear us? Where are you? *Who* are you! And why don't you answer! Are you even there?"

As Athena let her heart's truth surge forth, the sun blossomed into its full golden disk before her, almost as wide as the horizon itself. Its light became almost too much to bear; the three friends squinted and raised their hands to protect their eyes. Some of the grass near the platform smouldered and caught fire.

The voices from the immensity rumbled out with the reply:

We are always with you; we are always near you.

"Then why don't you *do* something?" Athena demanded to know. "It's not enough to know that you're watching. What we need is your *help*!"

The surface of the sun churned and boiled, as the gods prepared their answer.

We gave to you the birdsong of the morning, and the unfolding flowers of spring.

And in the white heat of the sun, Athena saw them: cardinals, chickadees, and warblers perched on fruit trees, nuthatches and finches collecting berries in the bushes, bees climbing into daffodils and celandines – all around the world.

We made for you the meadows and hills, the scented breeze in the forest, and the rainbow after the storm.

Athena found herself upon a hillside meadow, the edge of a forest to her back, and a spectacle of green hills and valleys rolling before her. The sun was warming her arms and legs and a gentle wind was swishing the leaves and wildflowers, bringing the richness of the loam to the air. All things were glistening from a recent rain.

We have spread upon the world everything you need to remember and renew the original goodness of your natures, and to mend what may be broken between you.

Athena beheld a kitchen table, where a family sat to enjoy a dinner prepared by everyone working together. A trio of dancers on a stage, performing with a small orchestra, before a delighted audience. An artist in a studio, painting a beloved's portrait. A nurse by an injured friend's side, examining and dressing the wound. A scholar in a library, with three books open on the table, making furious notes in a fourth with a quill. Two lovers entwined in the bliss of their bed, kissing and caressing each other.

It falls to you, working together, to find them, to use them well, and to care for them.

The gods returned her to the platform between the obelisks. Her friends were by her side, and the sun returned to his familiar size and place in the sky. Athena could hear the crashing of the ocean upon the cliff, far below.

We can do no more. For we are as lonely and poorly as you, under the aspect of eternity.

§ 51.

The three Summerlanders trudged in silence back to the *Sun Dog*. Each of them turned over in their minds the message from the gods, wondering if the moment was right to say something about it.

"So, it's up to us, then?" said Layla, when she could bear the silence no longer.

They walked a little further.

"And we had to come all this way, and Sylvano had to die, to find that out?" she added, with a sharpness in her voice. "It feels like too much. Like, we deserved something more."

A few more steps over a small rocky knoll.

Wicklow said, "No... I think I understand it. The gods don't want our obedience. They don't even want our worship. They want... something else. I'm not sure. Maybe I *don't* understand."

"Athena?" Layla asked, turning and stopping to face her friend.

Athena, her face long and lost in her own thoughts, carried on walking.

"Athena!" Layla said again.

Athena stopped and turned. She took a slow breath, preparing to speak. But she could not find the words. She regarded her friends for a long while, thanking them with her gaze for sharing the journey with her, yet also apologizing for it. The gods had answered her question, yet they left her with more questions. The reward for completing the quest was a continuation of the quest, something she could not expect, yet something she ought to have known.

She turned and carried on walking. Her friends soon followed at a respectful distance, gathering their thoughts in the sacred silence of the morning.

They came to the berth of the *Sun Dog*, still leaning on its side on the heather-dressed heath, its hull damaged from the landing, and its supplies spilled on the ground. Not quite a shipwreck, but no golden galleon. The apotheosis of their adventure.

They gathered the spilled supplies back onto the deck and lit the ethereal dynamo. The ship soon righted itself and rose into the air. More of the boards and planks creaked and strained than they had before, and the wind did not quite fill her sails.

Yet she flew.

Some distance away, half-hidden by a small patch of tallgrasses and heather, Dubhdarra watched them fly.

§ 52.

The gods intended Summerland to be beautiful. A place of safety and peace for everyone; a sheltered harbour in the endless cosmic ocean.

For nothing resisted the darkness so well as the crafting and sharing of beauty. The gods therefore planted the seeds of it everywhere, finding delight where they grew.

One seed fell into a maelstrom of stars, where it became a world. The gods perceived its goodness and came down to encourage its flourishing.

The first to arrive gave her flesh to be the soil, her blood to be the rivers, her breath to be the wind. She came to be called the Great Queen, wisest and most eldritch of the gods. And she named the new world Summerland.

Next came Green-maiden, who planted the grass, the flowers, the trees. Then Wild-father, who made all the animals. Sea-walker, who made the creatures of the ocean. And Golden-love, who made the colours of the twilight and the dawn. Thousands of gods came to Summerland in those distant early days, each with a gift to share.

And the Great Queen perceived: as her world changed and grew, it became more delicate and fragile. So, she gave birth to a son, and charged him to care for her world, to see to its health and integrity.

But the son looked into eternity, and feared what might lie in its darkness without end. Therefore, he created a race of warriors to protect Summerland. And he called these warriors Humans. He endowed his children with strength so they would be effective, intelligence so they would be adaptable, and spirit so they would be courageous. And in the language of the gods he named himself Ar'vanor, Maker of Kings.

The Queen smiled upon the young humans, and loved them as a grandmother. Yet she also perceived that if they had no other purpose but fighting, they would soon be a danger to Summerland, as well as to each other. Thus, she gave birth to two more children, a twin brother and sister, and charged them to teach humanity to be wise, and to love each other.

But the Twins also looked into eternity. They saw how the humans could grow in their power, enough to surpass all the gods. Thus, they devised a gambit to keep the gods in power above, and the mortals divided below. Instead of wisdom, the brother taught hatred and pride: he named himself Trézaar, The Victor And The Winner. And instead of love, the daughter taught vanity and lies: she took the name Vaska, The Blade Beneath The Velvet.

Some of the mortals took those poisons and found them sweet. They became the first of the tyrant-kings.

Some say the Queen creates new gods even now, charging them to counter the gambit of the Twins. And the Twins work to turn the new gods to their side, to continue to keep mortals down.

If we had a lifetime to tell their stories, we could not tell them all. For the world is vast, the gods are many, and magic awaits everywhere: the strange, the dark, and the wonderful, together.

§ 53.

"We can't tell anyone what the gods told us," Athena said, breaking a silence she had kept all day, as they ate their evening meal together.

"We have to say *something*," said Layla. "May as well tell the truth. Easier than lying."

"Will anyone want to hear it?" Athena asked. "Everybody back home thinks people are selfish asses, and we'd all turn into tyrant-kings if given half a chance. But if we told everyone that *the gods themselves* told us different, they'd say we're being foolish and naive. Or that we're lying to them. Nobody will believe us."

Layla said, "Then we tell them we found a few more Dawnlandic gazelles, and that's all. It's true, anyway. We got thirty pelts down below."

"Then they'd want to know where we found them," Wicklow said. "They might want me to help them get more."

"All the more reason to keep our story secret," Athena said. "In fact, after all we've seen and heard and done, I don't know how we can go home at all. But I think we *have* to. Someone has to stand up for the original goodness of the world. Someone has to insist that it's really there. And if not us, then who?"

This gave Layla an idea. "Maybe, when we go home, "she said, "we can look for people who need our help. People who had too much taken from them, and they feel like there's nothing they can do. We can bring them gifts in the night. Or we can help them escape. Whatever they need."

"Maybe, we also find out who is making the world uglier," said Wicklow. "And we mess with them a little. Just enough so they stop doing it."

"You're suggesting we become vigilantes?" Layla said, intrigued. "Start a little Movement of our own?"

"We're already outlaws," Wicklow said. "But now we're outlaws with a jackpot of money."

The three friends perked up. They smiled. They laughed.

"I like this plan – let's drink to it," said Athena. She poured wine for everyone and raised her cup to propose the toast: "Here's to all our future shenanigans!"

Layla raised her cup. "Summerland calls," she declared.

"And we shall rise," her friends replied with joy.

They clapped their cups together and drank. Their laughter carried on the wind and rose to the stars.

§ 54.

The flock of swallows swooped down from the sky, circled the mouth of a hollow hedgerow between two fields of barley. They converged and became Dubhdarra, with his ranger gear, his scarf, and his walking stick. He ambled down the sunken road inside the hedgerow. The overhanging branches were thick enough to make it like a tunnel into the earth. At its end lay his cottage, hidden in a small forest and perched on the top of a steep and high slope above a lake.

A winged rabbit hopped out of the undergrowth. Dubhdarra gave his friend a handful of food from one of his belt pouches. "Good evening, my friend," he said. "Sorry I was away for so long this time."

In his cottage, he hung up his belts, his weapons, and his armour. He piled some kindling into a pit in his yard and ignited it to flame with sparks struck by snapping his fingers. He hung a kettle on the chain over the fire, to boil water for his tea. Then he sat on an old wicker chair and put his feet up, to enjoy the view of the lake. The witch-rabbit hopped on to his lap and nuzzled his arms. The air cooled as twilight fell. A mist rose from the water and curled about the trees that clung to the slopes around the shore.

I trust you are satisfied with what became of Athena Kildare?

"Yes, indeed. I think she and her friends are off to a wonderful start," Dubhdarra replied, as he sipped his tea. "In fact, I plan to watch them for a little while longer. From a distance, of course. I still believe they've an important place in what's coming."

I agree. But do not neglect your other charges. Summerland shall soon need more friends.

The mist continued to rise from the lake, forming low clouds, and putting Dubhdarra into a contemplative mood.

"I have someone in mind already, who I'd like to visit next."

[end]

Author's Notes

Most of the time, when I write a novel, I begin with a character, a philosophical question, and a problem in that character's world which somehow reflects the question. This time, I began with a map. I drew it with a pencil on a sheet of newsprint, almost a meter wide, then traced elevation lines, rivers, lakes, settlements, roads, and islands. Then I gave them names. It was a surprisingly pleasurable exercise.

I drew the map some six years ago for a different project; one which, as it turned out, the map did not fit. But in those years, I re-traced it several times, re-arranged and re-named its features, and re-imagined the kind of ecosystems and climates its different provinces might host. It soon felt as familiar to me as the neighbourhood around my home. I knew it had stories to tell.

The map became the setting for a tabletop RPG, *Aeronauts and Musketeers*, which imagined a fairy-tale fantasy world undergoing a democratic revolution. But I wish to assure the reader that I intend for this novel to stand on its own. It is not the chronicle of a game session, and you don't need to study the game (nor the map) to understand the story here.

It was in the early months of 2023, a good friend told me that her fourteen-year-old daughter enjoyed two of my other novels and wanted to read more. I asked her to give me a few writing prompts. Does she have a favourite animal? What's a part of the world she'd like to visit some day? And so on. As her answers tumbled about in my mind, they became a story.

No one, or almost no one, considers the Swashbuckler a philosophical kind of literature. But if children's books can have adult philosophical themes in them – numerous contemporary children's authors have done this with great success – then I can write a philosophical swashbuckler. Or I can attempt it! The problem of evil is one such theme. There's something elemental about it, as though it's there to be discovered by anyone who thinks deeply enough about the ethics and religion. It's older than Christianity by some three centuries. But I've met teenage college students who came up with it all on their own. I've also never found a solution which satisfied me. The solution offered here rests upon a conception of the divine that you won't likely find in a Christian account of the problem, and it's not just the polytheism that makes the difference. I trust that you can pick it out from the story.

Finally, although Summerland is a hand-drawn map on a sheet of newsprint, it is also a place in my heart. I hope it is also a place in yours, if perhaps under a different name. And while it is a place where struggle and conflict abound, still it is a place where beauty, knowledge, and friendship endure. I think it is a terrible tragedy that most people stop dreaming of happier and more loving worlds when they become adults. If for no other reason: when we stop ourselves from imagining better worlds, we also diminish our capacity to imagine that our real world could be better, too. And thereby, we enervate the struggle to better it.

Brendan Myers

Krenicna, Central Bohemia, Czech Republic

July 2023.

www.ingramcontent.com/pod-product-compliance
Lightning Source LLC
Chambersburg PA
CBHW072137170626
46813CB00004BA/1594

* 9 7 8 1 7 7 7 8 5 8 9 4 0 *